MORE WILLIAM

Richmal Crompton was born in Lancashire in 1890. The first story about William Brown appeared in *Home* magazine in 1919, and the first collection of William stories was published in book form three years later. In all, thirty-eight William books were published, the last one in 1970, after Richmal Crompton's death.

'Probably the funniest, toughest children's books ever written'
Sunday Times on the Just William series

'Richmal Crompton's creation [has] been famed for his cavalier attitude to life and those who would seek to circumscribe his enjoyment of it ever since he first appeared'
Guardian

Books available in the Just William series

Just William
More William
William Again
William the Fourth
Still William
William the Conqueror
William the Outlaw
William in Trouble
William the Good
William at War

MORE
WILLIAM

RICHMAL CROMPTON

FOREWORD BY MARTIN JARVIS

ILLUSTRATED BY THOMAS HENRY

MACMILLAN CHILDREN'S BOOKS

First published in 1922
This selection first published 1995 by Macmillan Children's Books

This edition published 2010 by Macmillan Children's Books
a division of Macmillan Publishers Limited
20 New Wharf Road, London N1 9RR
Basingstoke and Oxford
Associated companies throughout the world
www.panmacmillan.com

ISBN 978-0-330-53535-9

5 7 9 8 6 4

A CIP catalogue record for this book is available from
the British Library.

Printed and bound by CPI Group (UK) Ltd, Croydon, CR0 4YY

CONTENTS

FOREWORD

More William? Yes, please.

This is one of the funniest books I've ever read. When I was recording it for BBC Audio a few years ago there were times when I could hardly keep going, simply because of the situations in which William gets embroiled and the brilliant hilarity of Richmal Crompton's writing. I'd be hooting with laughter and have to start a paragraph all over again. Then, just when I thought I'd regained some semblance of professional control, I'd glance up from the microphone, only to see the studio engineer and my co-producer doubled up with mirth on the other side of the glass . . . which would set me off once more. Exquisite agony!

Richmal Crompton was a hugely popular author: her timeless brainchild, eleven-year-old William Brown, was certainly the Harry Potter of the 1920s. Children, and parents, would wait anxiously for William's latest adventures before pouncing on them and racing away to devour more exploits of their lateral-thinking hero.

William's magic lies in his own personality, uniquely endowed by the generous genius of his creator. It's true that some of the starchier folk in William's village consider him mischievous, naughty, probably mendacious. His long-suffering family can think of even less flattering words to describe him. But we know that William pretty well always sets out with good intentions. It's just that, being him, things often go wrong; though, as in 'The May King' or 'William and the Smuggler', they can go surprisingly, gloriously right.

His motto invariably is 'Doin good, ritin' rongs and persuin' happiness for all'. Not a bad motive for life in any generation, let alone a world recovering from the staggering tragedies of World War I. 'Let me show you a good time,' William seems to say. 'It's jus' over there.' He's keen to bring justice (as he sees it) to an often unjust world, to prick the bubble of pomposity and, as the dance bands of the 1920s were already expressing in musical terms, to paint the clouds with sunshine.

Here, in this joyous book, William is at his

imaginative best. Whether he's conjuring up a ghost to give a batty aunt a spiritual thrill, attempting (with unexpected results) to assist a team of removal men or airily offering the hospitality of his home to a tramp with no ears, it's all approached with an utmost seriousness of purpose that can only result in laugh-out-loud comedy.

Crompton's world is still real, still recognizable, reflecting both the absurdity and blessedness of British life. William, though of his time, is for all time. Throughout Richmal Crompton's long writing career, until her death in 1969, William, always aged eleven, celebrated many birthdays and Christmases, righted numerous wrongs and brought much happiness to generations of fans. He still does.

William Brown's voice resonates down the years. Surely he's telling us, even now: 'Seems to me those people who keep sayin' I'm scruffy or a scamp, or worse – an' want to see and hear *less* of me – well, they'd better read this book, that's all I can say. S'jolly funny, an' it's all about me. S'called *More William*, not less, an' – ackshully – that's the way I like it.'

CHAPTER I

A BUSY DAY

William awoke and rubbed his eyes. It was Christmas Day – the day to which he had looked forward with mingled feelings for twelve months. It was a jolly day, of course – presents and turkey and crackers and staying up late. On the other hand, there were generally too many relations about, too much was often expected of one, the curious taste displayed by people who gave one presents often marred one's pleasure.

He looked round his bedroom expectantly. On the wall, just opposite his bed, was a large illuminated card hanging by a string from a nail – 'A Busy Day is a Happy Day'. That had not been there the day before. Brightly coloured roses and forget-me-nots and honeysuckle twined round all the words. William hastily thought over the three aunts staying in the house, and put it down to Aunt Lucy. He looked at it with a doubtful frown. He distrusted the sentiment.

A copy of *Portraits of our Kings and Queens* he put aside as beneath contempt. *Things a Boy Can Do* was more promising. *Much* more promising. After inspecting a penknife, a pocket compass, and a pencil box (which shared the fate of *Portraits of our Kings and Queens*), William returned to *Things a Boy Can Do*. As he turned the pages, his face lit up.

He leapt lightly out of bed and dressed. Then he began to arrange his own gifts to his family. For his father he had bought a bottle of highly coloured sweets, for his elder brother Robert (aged nineteen) he had expended a vast sum of money on a copy of *The Pirates of the Bloody Hand*. These gifts had cost him much thought. The knowledge that his father never touched sweets, and that Robert professed scorn of pirate stories, had led him to hope that the recipients of his gifts would make no objection to the unobtrusive theft of them by their recent donor in the course of the next few days. For his grown-up sister Ethel he had bought a box of coloured chalks. That also might come in useful later. Funds now had been running low, but for his mother he had bought a small cream jug which, after fierce bargaining, the man had let him have at half price because it was cracked.

Singing 'Christians, Awake!' at the top of his lusty young voice, he went along the landing, putting his gifts outside the doors of his family, and pausing to yell

'Happy Christmas' as he did so. From within he was greeted in each case by muffled groans.

He went downstairs into the hall, still singing. It was earlier than he thought – just five o'clock. The maids were not down yet. He switched on lights recklessly, and discovered that he was not the only person in the hall. His four-year-old cousin Jimmy was sitting on the bottom step in an attitude of despondency, holding an empty tin.

Jimmy's mother had influenza at home, and Jimmy and his small sister Barbara were in the happy position of spending Christmas with relations, but immune from parental or maternal interference.

'They've gotten out,' said Jimmy, sadly. 'I got 'em for presents yesterday, an' they've gotten out. I've been feeling for 'em in the dark, but I can't find 'em.'

'What?' said William.

'Snails. Great big suge ones wiv great big suge shells. I put 'em in a tin for presents an' they've gotten out an' I've gotten no presents for nobody.'

He relapsed into despondency.

William surveyed the hall.

'They've got out right enough!' he said, sternly. 'They've got out right *enough*. Jus' look at our hall! Jus' look at our clothes! They've got out *right* enough.'

Innumerable slimy iridescent trails shone over hats, and coats, and umbrellas, and wallpaper.

'Huh!' grunted William, who was apt to overwork his phrases. 'They got *out* right enough.'

He looked at the tracks again and brightened. Jimmy was frankly delighted.

'Oo! Look!' he cried. 'Oo *funny*!'

William's thought flew back to his bedroom wall – 'A Busy Day is a Happy Day'.

'Let's clean it up!' he said. 'Let's have it all nice an' clean for when they come down. We'll be busy. You tell me if you feel happy when we've done. It might be true wot it says, but I don't like the flowers messin' all over it.'

Investigation in the kitchen provided them with a large pail of water and scrubbing brush each.

For a long time they worked in silence. They used plenty of water. When they had finished the trails were all gone. Each soaked garment on the hatstand was sending a steady drip on to the already flooded floor. The wallpaper was sodden. With a feeling of blankness they realised that there was nothing else to clean.

It was Jimmy who conceived the exquisite idea of dipping his brush in the bucket and sprinkling William with water. A scrubbing brush is in many ways almost as good as a hose. Each had a pail of ammunition. Each had a good-sized brush. During the next few minutes they experienced purest joy. Then William heard threatening movements above, and decided hastily that the battle must cease.

'Backstairs,' he said shortly. 'Come on.'

Marking their track by a running stream of water, they crept up the backstairs.

But two small boys soaked to the skin could not disclaim all knowledge of a flooded hall.

William was calm and collected when confronted with a distracted mother.

'We was tryin' to clean up,' he said. 'We found all snail marks an' we was tryin' to clean up. We was tryin' to help. You said so last night, you know, when you was talkin' to me. You said to *help*. Well, I thought it was helpin' to try an' clean up. You can't clean up with water an' not get wet – not if you do it prop'ly. You said to try an' make Christmas Day happy for other folks and then I'd be happy. Well, I don't know as I'm very happy,' he said, bitterly, 'but I've been workin' hard enough since early this mornin'. I've been workin',' he went on pathetically. His eye wandered to the notice on his wall. 'I've been *busy* all right, but it doesn't make me *happy* – not jus' now,' he added, with memories of the rapture of the fight. That certainly must be repeated some time. Buckets of water and scrubbing brushes. He wondered he'd never thought of that before.

William's mother looked down at his dripping form.

'Did you get all that water with just cleaning up the snail marks?' she said.

William coughed and cleared his throat. 'Well,' he said, deprecatingly, 'most of it. I think I got most of it.'

'If it wasn't Christmas Day . . .' she went on darkly.

William's spirits rose. There was certainly something to be said for Christmas Day.

It was decided to hide the traces of the crime as far as possible from William's father. It was felt – and not without reason – that William's father's feelings of respect for the sanctity of Christmas Day might be overcome by his feelings of paternal ire.

Half an hour later William, dried, dressed, brushed, and chastened, descended the stairs as the gong sounded in a hall which was bare of hats and coats, and whose floor shone with cleanliness.

'And jus to think,' said William, despondently, 'that it's only jus' got to brekfust time.'

William's father was at the bottom of the stairs. William's father frankly disliked Christmas Day.

'Good morning, William,' he said, 'and a happy

Christmas, and I hope it's not too much to ask of you that on this relation-infested day one's feelings may be harrowed by you as little as possible. And why the deu— dickens they think it necessary to wash the hall floor before breakfast, heaven only knows!'

William coughed, a cough meant to be a polite mixture of greeting and deference. William's face was a study in holy innocence. His father glanced at him suspiciously. There were certain expressions of William's that he distrusted.

William entered the dining-room morosely. Jimmy's sister Barbara – a small bundle of curls and white frills – was already beginning her porridge.

'Goo' mornin',' she said, politely, 'did you hear me cleanin' my teef?'

He crushed her with a glance.

He sat eating in silence till everyone had come down, and Aunts Jane, Evangeline, and Lucy were consuming porridge with that mixture of festivity and solemnity that they felt the occasion demanded.

Then Jimmy entered, radiant, with a tin in his hand.

'Got presents,' he said, proudly. 'Got presents, lots of presents.'

He deposited on Barbara's plate a worm which Barbara promptly threw at his face. Jimmy looked at her reproachfully and proceeded to Aunt Evangeline. Aunt Evangeline's gift was a centipede – a live centipede that ran gaily off the tablecloth on to Aunt Evangeline's lap before anyone could stop it. With a yell that sent William's father to the library with his hands to his ears, Aunt Evangeline leapt to her chair and stood with her skirts held to her knees.

'Help! Help!' she cried. 'The horrible boy! Catch it! Kill it!'

Jimmy gazed at her in amazement, and Barbara looked with interest at Aunt Evangeline's long expanse of shin.

'*My* legs isn't like *your* legs,' she said pleasantly and conversationally. 'My legs is knees.'

It was some time before order was restored, the centipede killed, and Jimmy's remaining gifts thrown out of the window. William looked across the table at Jimmy with respect in his eye. Jimmy, in spite of his youth, was an acquaintance worth cultivating. Jimmy was eating porridge unconcernedly.

Aunt Evangeline had rushed from the room when the slaughter of the centipede had left the coast clear, and refused to return. She carried on a conversation from the top of the stairs.

'When that horrible child has gone, I'll come in. He

may have insects concealed on his person. And someone's been dropping water all over these stairs. They're
damp!'

'Dear, dear!' murmured Aunt Jane, sadly.

Jimmy looked up from his porridge.

'How was I to know she didn't like insecks?' he said,
aggrievedly. '*I* like 'em.'

William's mother's despair was only tempered by the
fact that this time William was not the culprit. To
William also it was a novel sensation. He realised the
advantages of a fellow criminal.

After breakfast peace reigned. William's father went
out for a walk with Robert. The aunts sat round the
drawing-room fire talking and doing crochet work. In
this consists the whole art and duty of aunthood. *All*
aunts do crochet work.

They had made careful inquiries about the time of
the service.

'You needn't worry,' had said William's mother. 'It's
at ten thirty, and if you go to get ready when the clock
in the library strikes ten it will give you heaps of time.'

Peace . . . calm . . . quiet. Mrs Brown and Ethel in the
kitchen supervising the arrangements for the day. The
aunts in the drawing-room discussing over their crochet
work the terrible way in which their sisters had brought

up their children. That, also, is a necessary part of aunt-hood.

Time slipped by happily and peacefully. Then William's mother came into the drawing-room.

'I thought you were going to church,' she said.

'We are. The clock hasn't struck.'

'But – it's eleven o'clock!'

There was a gasp of dismay.

'The clock never struck!'

Indignantly they set off to the library. Peace and quiet reigned also in the library. On the floor sat William and Jimmy gazing with frowns of concentration at an open page of *Things a Boy Can Do*. Around them lay most indecently exposed the internal arrangements of the library clock.

'William! You *wicked* boy!'

William raised a frowning face.

'It's not put together right,' he said; 'it's not been put together right all this time. We're makin' it right now. It must have wanted mendin' for ever so long. *I* dunno how it's been goin' at all. It's lucky we found it out. It's put together wrong. I guess it's *made* wrong. It's goin' to be a lot of trouble to us to put it right, an' we can't do much when you're all standin' in the light. We're very busy – workin' at tryin' to mend this ole clock for you all.'

AROUND THEM LAY, MOST INDECENTLY EXPOSED, THE
INTERNAL ARRANGEMENTS OF THE LIBRARY CLOCK.

'Clever,' said Jimmy, admiringly. 'Mendin' the clock. *Clever!*'

'William!' groaned his mother. 'You've ruined the clock. What *will* your father say?'

'Well, the cog wheels was wrong,' said William doggedly. 'See? An' this ratchet-wheel isn't on the pawl prop'ly – not like what this book says it ought to be. Seems we've got to take it all to pieces to get it right. Seems to me the person wot made this clock didn't know much about clock-making. Seems to me—'

'Be *quiet*, William!'

'We was be quietin' 'fore you came in,' said Jimmy severely. 'You 'sturbed us.'

'Leave it just as it is, William,' said his mother.

'You don't *unnerstand*,' said William with the excitement of the fanatic. 'The cog wheel an' the ratchet ought to be put on the arbor different. See, this is the cog wheel. Well, it oughtn't to be like wot it was. It was put on all *wrong*. Well, we was mendin' it. An' we was doin' it for *you*,' he ended, bitterly, 'jus' to help an' – to – to make other folks happy. It makes folks happy havin' clocks goin' right, anyone would *think*. But if you *want* your clocks put together wrong, *I* don't care.'

He picked up his book and walked proudly from the room followed by the admiring Jimmy.

'William,' said Aunt Lucy patiently, as he passed, 'I don't want to say anything unkind, and I hope you won't remember all your life that you have completely spoilt this Christmas Day for me.'

'Oh, dear!' murmured Aunt Jane, sadly.

William, with a look before which she should have sunk into the earth, answered shortly that he didn't think he would.

During the midday dinner the grown-ups, as is the foolish fashion of grown-ups, wasted much valuable time in the discussion of such futilities as the weather and the political state of the nation. Aunt Lucy was still suffering and aggrieved.

'I can go this evening, of course,' she said, 'but it's not quite the same. The morning service is different. Yes, please, dear – *and* stuffing. Yes, I'll have a little more turkey, too. And, of course, the Vicar may not preach tonight. That makes such a difference. The gravy on the potatoes, please. It's almost the first Christmas I've not been in the morning. It seems quite to have spoilt the day for me.'

She bent on William a glance of gentle reproach. William was quite capable of meeting adequately that or any other glance, but at present he was too busy for minor hostilities. He was *extremely* busy. He was doing his utmost to do full justice to a meal that only happens once a year.

'William,' said Barbara pleasantly, 'I can *dweam*. Can you?'

He made no answer.

'Answer your cousin, William,' said his mother.

He swallowed, then spoke plaintively. 'You always say not to talk with my mouth full,' he said.

'You could speak when you've finished the mouthful.'

'Dear, *dear*!' murmured Aunt Jane.

This was Aunt Jane's usual contribution to any conversation.

He looked coldly at the three pairs of horrified aunts' eyes around him, then placidly continued his meal.

Mrs Brown hastily changed the subject of conversation. The art of combining the duties of mother and hostess is sometimes a difficult one.

Christmas afternoon is a time of rest. The three aunts withdrew from public life. Aunt Lucy found a book of sermons in the library and retired to her bedroom with it.

'It's the next best thing, I think,' she said with a sad glance at William.

William was beginning definitely to dislike Aunt Lucy.

'Please'm,' said the cook an hour later, 'the mincing machine's disappeared.'

'Disappeared?' said William's mother, raising her hand to her head.

'Clean gone'm. 'Ow'm I to get the supper'm? You said as 'ow I could get it done this afternoon so as to go to church this evening. I can't do nuffink with the mincing machine gone.'

'I'll come and look.'

They searched every corner of the kitchen, then William's mother had an idea. William's mother had not been William's mother for eleven years without learning many things. She went wearily up to William's bedroom.

William was sitting on the floor. Open beside him was *Things a Boy Can Do*. Around him lay various parts of the mincing machine. His face was set and strained in mental and physical effort. He looked up as she entered.

'It's a funny kind of mincing machine,' he said, crushingly. 'It's not got enough parts. It's *made* wrong—'

'Do you know,' she said, slowly, 'that we've all been

looking for that mincing machine for the last half-hour?'

'No,' he said without much interest, 'I di'n't. I'd have told you I was mendin' it if you'd told me you was lookin' for it. It's *wrong*,' he went on aggrievedly. 'I can't make anything with it. Look! It says in my book "How to make a model railway signal with parts of a mincing machine". Listen! It says, "Borrow a mincing machine from your mother——"'

'Did you borrow it?' said Mrs Brown.

'Yes. Well, I've got it, haven't I? I went all the way down to the kitchen for it.'

'Who lent it to you?'

'No one *lent* it to me. I *borrowed* it. I thought you'd like to see a model railway signal. I thought you'd be interested. Anyone would think anyone would be interested in seein' a railway signal made out of a mincin' machine.'

His tone implied that the dullness of people in general was simply beyond him. 'An' you haven't got a right sort of mincin' machine. It's wrong. Its parts are the wrong shape. I've been hammerin' them, tryin' to make them right, but they're *made* wrong.'

Mrs Brown was past expostulating. 'Take them all down to the kitchen to Cook,' she said. 'She's waiting for them.'

On the stairs William met Aunt Lucy carrying her volume of sermons.

'It's not quite the same as the spoken word, William dear,' she said. 'It hasn't the *force*. The written word doesn't reach the *heart* as the spoken word does, but I don't want you to worry about it.'

William walked on as if he had not heard her.

It was Aunt Jane who insisted on the little entertainment after tea.

'I *love* to hear the dear children recite,' she said. 'I'm sure they all have some little recitation they can say.'

Barbara arose with shy delight to say her piece.

Lickle bwown seed, lickle bwown bwother,
And what, pway, are you goin' to be?
I'll be a poppy as white as my mother,
Oh, DO be a poppy like me!
What, you'll be a sunflower? Oh, how I shall
    miss you
When you are golden and high!
But I'll send all the bees up to tiss you.
Lickle bwown bwother, goodbye!

She sat down blushing, amid rapturous applause.

Next Jimmy was dragged from his corner. He stood

up as one prepared for the worst, shut his eyes, and –

Licklaxokindness lickledeedsolove –
make – thisearfanedenliketheeav'nabovethasalliknow.

He gasped it all in one breath, and sat down panting.

This was greeted with slightly milder applause.

'Now, William!'

'I don't know any,' he said.

'Oh, you *do*,' said his mother. 'Say the one you learnt at school last term. Stand up, dear, and speak clearly.'

Slowly William rose to his feet.

'*It was the schooner Hesperus that sailed the wintry*
sea,'

he began.

Here he stopped, coughed, cleared his throat, and began again.

It was the schooner Hesperus that sailed the wintry
sea.

'Oh, get *on*!' muttered his brother, irritably.

'I can't get on if you keep talkin' to me,' said William sternly. 'How can I get on if you keep takin' all the time up, *sayin'* get on? I can't get on if you're talkin', can I?'

'It was the Hesper Schoonerus that sailed the wintry sea an' I'm not goin' on if Ethel's goin' to keep gigglin'. It's not a funny piece, an' if she's goin' on gigglin' like that I'm not sayin' any more of it.'

'Ethel, dear!' murmured Mrs Brown, reproachfully.

'IT WAS THE HESPER SCHOONERUS THAT SAILED THE WINTRY SEA AN' I'M NOT GOIN' ON IF ETHEL'S GOIN' TO KEEP GIGGLIN'.'

Ethel turned her chair completely round and left only her back exposed to William's view. He glared at it suspiciously.

'Now, William, dear,' continued his mother, 'begin again and no one shall interrupt you.'

William again went through the preliminaries of coughing and clearing his throat.

It was the schooner Hesperus that sailed the wintry seas.

He stopped again, and slowly and carefully straightened his collar and smoothed back the lock of hair which was dangling over his brow.

'*The skipper had brought*—' prompted Aunt Jane, kindly.

William turned on her.

'I was *goin'* to say that if you'd left me alone,' he said. 'I was jus' thinkin'. I've got to think sometimes. I can't say off a great long pome like that without stoppin' to think sometimes, can I? I'll – I'll do a conjuring trick for you instead,' he burst out, desperately. 'I've learnt one from my book. I'll go an' get it ready.'

He went out of the room. Mr Brown took out his handkerchief and mopped his brow.

'May I ask,' he said patiently, 'how long this exhibition is to be allowed to continue?'

Here William returned, his pockets bulging. He held a large handkerchief in his hand.

'This is a handkerchief,' he announced. 'If anyone'd like to feel it to see if it's a real one, they can. Now I want a shilling.' He looked round expectantly, but no one moved. 'Or a penny would do,' he said, with a slightly disgusted air. Robert threw one across the room. 'Well, I put the penny into the handkerchief. You can see me do it, can't you? If anyone wants to come an' feel the penny is in the handkerchief, they can. Well,' he turned his back on them and took something out of his pocket. After a few contortions he turned round again, holding the handkerchief tightly. 'Now, you look close' – he went over to them – 'an' you'll see the shil— I mean, penny,' he looked scornfully at Robert, 'has changed to an egg. It's a real egg. If anyone thinks it isn't a real egg—'

But it *was* a real egg. It confirmed his statement by giving a resounding crack and sending a shining stream partly on to the carpet and partly on to Aunt Evangeline's black silk knee. A storm of reproaches burst out.

'First that horrible insect,' almost wept Aunt Evangeline, 'and then this messy stuff all over me. It's a good

21

thing I don't live here. One day a year is enough . . . My
nerves! . . .'

'Dear, dear!' said Aunt Jane.

'Fancy taking a new-laid *egg* for that,' said Ethel
severely.

William was pale and indignant.

'Well, I did jus' what the book said to do. Look at it.
It says: "Take an egg. Conceal it in the pocket." Well, I
took an egg an' I concealed it in the pocket. Seems to
me,' he said bitterly, 'seems to me this book isn't *Things
a Boy Can Do*. It's *Things a Boy Can't Do*.'

Mr Brown rose slowly from his chair.

'You're just about right there, my son. Thank *you*,'
he said with elaborate politeness, as he took the book
from William's reluctant hands and went over with it to
a small cupboard in the wall. In this cupboard reposed
an airgun, a bugle, a catapult, and a mouth organ. As he
unlocked it to put the book inside, the fleeting glimpse
of his confiscated treasures added to the bitterness of
William's soul.

'On Christmas Day, too!'

While he was still afire with silent indignation Aunt
Lucy returned from church.

'The Vicar *didn't* preach,' she said. 'They say that
this morning's sermon was beautiful. As I say, I don't

want William to reproach himself, but I feel that he has deprived me of a very great treat.'

'*Nice* William!' murmured Jimmy sleepily from his corner.

As William undressed that night his gaze fell upon the flower-bedecked motto: 'A Busy Day is a Happy Day'.

'It's a story,' he said, indignantly. 'It's jus' a wicked ole story.

CHAPTER 2

RICE-MOULD

'Rice-mould,' said the little girl next door bitterly. 'Rice-mould! Rice-mould! Every single day. I *hate* it, don't you?'

She turned gloomy blue eyes upon William, who was perched perilously on the ivy-covered wall. William considered thoughtfully.

'Dunno,' he said. 'I just eat it; I never thought about it.'

'It's *hateful*, just *hateful*. Ugh! I've had it at dinner and I'll have it at supper – bet you anything. I say, you are going to have a party tonight, aren't you?'

William nodded carelessly.

'Are you going to be there?'

'Me!' ejaculated William in a tone of amused surprise. 'I should think so! You don't think they could have it without *me*, do you? Huh! Not much!'

She gazed at him enviously.

'You *are* lucky! I expect you'll have a lovely supper – not rice-mould,' she said bitterly.

'Rather!' said William with an air of superiority.

'What are you going to have to eat at your party?'

'Oh – everything,' said William vaguely.

'Cream blancmange?'

'Heaps of it – *buckets* of it.'

The little girl next door clasped her hands.

'Oh, just think of it! Your eating cream blancmange and me eating – *rice-mould*!' (It is impossible to convey in print the intense scorn and hatred which the little girl next door could compress into the two syllables.)

Here an idea struck William.

'What time do you have supper?'

'Seven.'

'Well, now,' magnanimously, 'if you'll be in your summer house at half past, I'll bring you some cream blancmange. Truly I will!'

The little girl's face beamed with pleasure.

'Will you? Will you *really*? You won't forget?'

'Not me! I'll be there. I'll slip away from our show on the quiet with it.'

'Oh, how *lovely*! I'll be thinking of it every minute. Don't forget. Goodbye.'

She blew him a kiss and flitted daintily into the house.

William blushed furiously at the blown kiss and descended from his precarious perch.

He went to the library where his grown-up sister Ethel and his elder brother Robert were standing on ladders at opposite ends of the room, engaged in hanging up festoons of ivy and holly across the wall. There was to be dancing in the library after supper. William's mother watched them from a safe position on the floor.

'Look here, mother,' began William. 'Am I or am I not coming to the party tonight?'

William's Mother sighed.

'For goodness sake, William, don't open that discussion again. For the tenth time today, you are *not*!'

'But *why* not?' he persisted. 'I only want to know why not. That's all I want to know. It looks a bit funny, doesn't it, to give a party and leave out your only son, at least' – with a glance at Robert, and a slight concession to accuracy – 'to leave out one of your only two sons? It looks a bit queer surely. That's all I'm thinking of – how it will look.'

'A bit higher your end,' said Ethel.

'Yes, that's better,' said William's mother.

'It's a *young* folks' party,' went on William, warming to his subject. 'I heard you tell Aunt Jane it was a *young* folks' party. Well, I'm young, aren't I? I'm eleven. Do you want me any younger? You aren't ashamed of folks seeing me, are you? I'm not deformed or anything.'

'IF YOU'LL BE IN YOUR SUMMER HOUSE AT HALF PAST, I'LL
BRING YOU SOME CREAM BLANCMANGE. TRULY I WILL!'
SAID WILLIAM.

'That's right! Put the nail in there, Ethel.'

'Just a bit higher. That's right!'

'P'raps you're afraid of what I'll *eat*,' went on William bitterly. 'Well, everyone eats, don't they? They've got to – to live. And you've got things for us – them – to eat tonight. You don't grudge me just a bit of supper, do you? You'd think it was less trouble for me to have my bit of supper with you all, than in a separate room. That's all I'm thinking of – the trouble—'

William's sister turned round on her ladder and faced the room.

'Can't *anyone*,' she said desperately, 'stop that child talking?'

William's brother began to descend the ladder. 'I think I can,' he said grimly.

But William had thrown dignity to the winds, and fled.

He went down the hall to the kitchen, where Cook hastily interposed herself between him and the table that was laden with cakes and jellies and other delicacies.

'Now, Master William,' she said sharply, 'you clear out of here!'

'I don't want any of your things, Cook,' said William, magnificently but untruthfully. 'I only came to see how you were getting on. That's all I came for.'

'We're getting on very well indeed, thank you, Master

William,' she said with sarcastic politeness, 'but nothing for you till tomorrow, when we can see how much they've left.'

She returned to her task of cutting sandwiches. William, from a respectful distance, surveyed the table with its enticing burden.

'Huh!' he ejaculated bitterly. 'Think of them sitting and stuffing, and stuffing, and stuffing away at *our* food all night! I don't suppose they'll leave much – not if I know the set that lives round here!'

'Don't judge them all by yourself, Master William,' said Cook unkindly, keeping a watchful eye upon him. 'Here, Emma, put that rice-mould away in the pantry. It's for tomorrow's lunch.'

Rice-mould! That reminded him.

'Cook,' he said ingratiatingly, 'are you going to make cream blancmange?'

'I am *not*, Master William,' she said firmly.

'Well,' he said, with a short laugh, 'it'll be a queer party without cream blancmange! I've never heard of a party without cream blancmange! They'll think it's a bit funny. No one ever gives a party round here without cream blancmange!'

'Don't they indeed, Master William,' said Cook, with ironic interest.

'No. You'll be making one, p'raps, later on – just a little one, won't you?'

'And why should I?'

'Well, I'd like to think they had a cream blancmange. I think they'd enjoy it. That's all I'm thinking of.'

'Oh, is it? Well, it's your ma that tells me what to make and pays me for it, not you.'

This was a novel idea to William.

He thought deeply.

'Look here!' he said at last. 'If I gave you' – he paused for effect, then brought out the startling offer – 'sixpence, would you make a cream blancmange?'

'I'd want to see your sixpence first,' said Cook, with a wink at Emma.

William retired upstairs to his bedroom and counted out his money – twopence was all he possessed. He had expended the enormous sum of a shilling the day before on a grass snake. It had died in the night. He *must* get a cream blancmange somehow. His reputation for omnipotence in the eyes of the little girl next door – a reputation very dear to him – depended on it. And if Cook would do it for sixpence, he must find sixpence. By fair means or foul it must be done. He'd tried fair means, and there only remained foul. He went softly downstairs to the dining-room, where, upon the mantelpiece, reposed the missionary box. He'd tell someone next day, or put it back, or something. Anyway, people did worse things than that in the pictures. With a knife from the table he extracted the contents – three halfpence! He glared at it balefully.

'Three halfpence!' he said aloud in righteous indignation. 'This is supposed to be a Christian house, and three halfpence is all they can give to the poor heathen. They can spend pounds and pounds on' – he glanced round the room and saw a pyramid of pears on the sideboard – 'tons of pears an' – an' green stuff to put on the walls, and they give three halfpence to the poor heathen! Huh!'

He opened the door and heard his sister's voice from the library. 'He's probably in mischief somewhere. He'll be a perfect nuisance all the evening. Mother, couldn't you make him go to bed an hour earlier?'

William had no doubt as to the subject of the conversation. *Make him go to bed early!* He'd like to see them! He'd just like to see them! And he'd show them, anyway. Yes, he would show them. Exactly what he would show them and how he would show them, he was not as yet very clear. He looked round the room again. There were no eatables in it so far except the piled-up plate of huge pears on the sideboard.

He looked at it longingly. They'd probably counted them and knew just how many there ought to be. Mean sort of thing they would do. And they'd be in counting them every other minute just to see if he'd taken one. Well, he was going to score off somebody, somehow. Make him go to bed early indeed! He stood with knit brows, deep in thought, then his face cleared and he smiled. He'd got it! For the next five minutes he munched the delicious pears, but, at the end, the piled-up pyramid was apparently exactly as he found it, not a pear gone, only – on the inner side of each pear, the side that didn't show, was a huge semicircular bite. William wiped his mouth with his coat sleeve. They were jolly good pears. And a blissful vision came to him of the faces of the guests as they took the pears, of the faces of his father and mother and Robert and Ethel. Oh, crumbs! He chuckled to himself as he went down to the kitchen again.

'I say, Cook, could you make a small one – quite a small one – for threepence-halfpenny?'

Cook laughed.

'I was only pulling your leg, Master William. I've got one made and locked up in the larder.'

'That's all right,' said William. 'I – wanted them to have a cream blancmange, that's all.'

'Oh, *they'll* have it all right; they won't leave much for you. I only made *one*!'

'Did you say locked in the larder?' said William carelessly. 'It must be a bother for you to *lock* the larder door each time you go in?'

'Oh, no trouble, Master William, thank you,' said Cook sarcastically; 'there's more than the cream blancmange there; there's pasties and cakes and other things. I'm thinking of the last party your ma gave!'

William had the grace to blush. On that occasion William and a friend had spent the hour before supper in the larder, and supper had to be postponed while fresh provisions were beaten up from any and every quarter. William had passed a troubled night and spent the next day in bed.

'Oh, *then*! That was a long time ago. I was only a kid then.'

'Umph!' grunted the cook. Then, relenting, 'Well, if there's any cream blancmange left I'll bring it up to you in bed. Now that's a promise. Here, Emma, put these sandwiches in the larder. Here's the key! Now mind you *lock it* after you!'

'Cook! Just come here for a minute.'

It was the voice of William's mother from the library. William's heart rose. With Cook away from the scene of action great things might happen. Emma took the dish of sandwiches, unlocked the pantry door, and entered.

There was a crash of crockery from the back kitchen. Emma fled out, leaving the door unlocked. After she had picked up several broken plates, which had unaccountably slipped from the shelves, she returned and locked the pantry door.

William, in the darkness within, heaved a sigh of relief. He was in, anyway; how he was going to get out he wasn't quite sure. He stood for a few minutes in rapt admiration of his own cleverness. He'd scored off Cook! Crumbs! He'd scored off Cook! So far, at any rate. The first thing to do was to find the cream blancmange. He found it at last and sat down with it on the bread pan to consider his next step.

Suddenly he became aware of two green eyes staring at him in the darkness. The cat was in too! Crumbs! The cat was in too! The cat, recognising its inveterate enemy, set up a vindictive wail. William grew cold with fright. The rotten old cat was going to give the show away!

'Here, Pussy! Good ole Pussy!' he whispered hoarsely. 'Nice ole Pussy! Good ole Pussy!'

The cat gazed at him in surprise. This form of address from William was unusual.

'Good ole Pussy!' went on William feverishly. 'Shut up, then. Here's some nice blancmange. Just have a bit. Go on, have a bit an shut up.'

He put the dish down on the larder floor before the cat, and the cat, after a few preliminary licks, decided that it was good. William sat watching for a bit. Then he came to the conclusion that it was no use wasting time, and began to sample the plates around him. He ate a whole jelly, and then took four sandwiches off each plate, and four cakes and pasties off each plate. He had learnt wisdom since the last party. Meanwhile, the cat licked away at the cream blancmange with every evidence of satisfaction. It even began to purr, and as its satisfaction increased so did the purr. It possessed a peculiar penetrating purr.

'Cook!' called out Emma from the kitchen.

Cook came out of the library where she was assisting with the festoon hanging. 'What's the matter?'

'There's a funny buzzing noise in the larder.'

'Well, go in and see what it is. It's probably a wasp, that's all.'

Emma approached with the key, and William, clasping the blancmange to his bosom, withdrew behind the door, slipping off his shoes in readiness for action.

'Poor Puss!' said Emma, opening the door and meeting the cat's green, unabashed gaze. 'Did it get shut up in the nasty dark larder, then? Who did it then?'

She was bending down with her back to William, stroking the cat in the doorway. William seized his chance.

He dashed past her and up the stairs in stockinged feet like a flash of lightning. But Emma, leaning over the cat, had espied a dark flying figure out of the corner of her eye. She set up a scream. Out of the library came William's mother, William's sister, William's brother and Cook.

'A burglar in the larder!' gasped Emma. 'I seed 'im, I did! Out of the corner of my eye, like, and when I looked up 'e wasn't there no more. Flittin' up the 'all like a shadder, 'e was. Oh, lor! It's fairly turned me inside! Oh, lor!'

'What rubbish!' said William's mother. 'Emma, you must control yourself.'

'I went into the larder myself, 'm,' said Cook indignantly, 'just before I came in to 'elp with the greenery ornaments, and it was hempty as – hair. It's all that silly Emma! Always 'avin' the jumps she is—'

'Where's William?' said William's mother with sudden suspicion. 'William!'

William came out of his bedroom and looked over the balusters.

'Yes, Mother,' he said, with that wondering innocence of voice and look which he had brought to a fine art, and which proved one of his greatest assets in times of stress and strain.

'What are you doing?'

'Jus' readin' quietly in my room, Mother.'

'Oh, for heaven's sake don't disturb him, then,' said William's sister.

'It's those silly books you read, Emma. You're always imagining things. If you'd read the ones I recommend instead of the foolish ones you will get hold of—'

William's mother was safely mounted on one of her favourite hobby horses. William withdrew to his room and carefully concealed the cream blancmange beneath his bed. He then waited till he heard the guests arrive and exchange greetings in the hall. William, listening with his door open, carefully committed to memory the voice and manner of his sister's greeting to her friends. That would come in useful later on, probably. No weapon of offence against the world in general and his own family in particular, was to be despised. He held a rehearsal in his room when the guests were all safely assembled in the drawing-room.

'Oh, *how* are you, Mrs Green?' he said in a high falsetto, meant to represent the feminine voice. 'And how's the *darling* baby? *Such* a duck! I'm dying to see him again! Oh, Delia, darling! There you are! *So* glad you could come! What a perfect darling of a dress, my dear. I know whose heart you'll break in that! Oh, Mr Thompson!' – here William languished, bridled and ogled in a fashion seen nowhere on earth except in his imitations of his sister when engaged in conversation with one of the male sex. If reproduced at the right moment, it was guaranteed to drive her to a frenzy: 'I'm *so* glad to see you. Yes, of course I really am! I wouldn't say it if I wasn't!'

The drawing-room door opened and a chatter of conversation and a rustling of dresses arose from the hall. Oh, crumbs! They were going in to supper. Yes, the dining-room door closed; the coast was clear. William took out the rather battered-looking delicacy from under the bed and considered it thoughtfully. The dish was big and awkwardly shaped. He must find something that would go under his coat better than that. He couldn't march through the hall and out of the front door, bearing a cream blancmange, naked and unashamed. And the back door through the kitchen was impossible. With infinite care but little success as far as the shape of the blancmange was concerned, he removed it from its dish on to his soap dish. He forgot, in the excitement of the moment, to remove the soap, but, after all, it was only a small piece. The soap dish was decidedly too small for it, but, clasped to William's bosom inside his coat, it could be partly supported by his arm outside. He descended the stairs cautiously. He tiptoed lightly past the dining-room door (which was slightly ajar), from which came the shrill, noisy, meaningless, conversation of the grown-ups. He was just about to open the front door when there came the sound of a key turning in the lock.

William's heart sank. He had forgotten the fact that his father generally returned from his office about this time.

William's father came into the hall and glanced at his youngest offspring suspiciously.

'Hello!' he said. 'Where are you going?'

William cleared his throat nervously.

'Me?' he questioned lightly. 'Oh, I was jus' – jus' goin' for a little walk up the road before I went to bed. That's all I was going to do, Father.'

Flop! A large segment of the cream blancmange had disintegrated itself from the fast-melting mass, and, evading William's encircling arm, had fallen on to the floor at his feet. With praiseworthy presence of mind William promptly stepped on to it and covered it with his feet. William's father turned round quickly from the stand where he was replacing his walking stick.

'What was that?'

William looked round the hall absently. 'What, Father?'

William's father now fastened his eyes upon William's person.

'What have you got under your coat?'

'Where?' said William with apparent surprise.

Then, looking down at the damp excrescence of his coat, as if he noticed it for the first time, 'Oh, that!' with a mirthless smile. 'Do you mean *that*? Oh, that's jus' – jus' somethin' I'm takin' out with me, that's all.'

Again William's father grunted.

'Well,' he said, 'if you're going for this walk up the road why on earth don't you go, instead of standing as if you'd lost the use of your feet?'

William's father was hanging up his overcoat with his back to William, and the front door was open. William wanted no second bidding. He darted out of the door and down the drive, but he was just in time to hear the thud of a falling body and to hear a muttered curse as the Head of the House entered the dining-room feet first on a long slide of some white, glutinous substance.

'Oh, crumbs!' gasped William as he ran.

The little girl next door was sitting in the summer house, armed with a spoon, when William arrived. His precious burden had now saturated his shirt and was striking cold and damp on his chest. He drew it from his coat and displayed it proudly. It had certainly lost its pristine, white, rounded appearance. The marks of the cat's licks were very evident; grime from William's coat adhered to its surface; it wobbled limply over the soap dish, but the little girl's eyes sparkled as she saw it.

'Oh, William, I never thought you really would! Oh, you are wonderful! And I *had* it!'

'What?'

'Rice-mould for supper, but I didn't mind, because I thought – I hoped, you'd come with it. Oh, William, you *are a nice* boy!'

William glowed with pride.

'William!' bellowed an irate voice from William's front door.

William knew that voice. It was the voice of the male parent who has stood all he's jolly well going to stand from that kid, and is out for vengeance. They'd got to the pears! Oh, crumbs! They'd got to the pears! And even the thought of Nemesis to come could not dull for William the bliss of that vision.

'Oh, William,' said the little girl next door sadly, 'they're calling you. Will you have to go?'

'Not me,' said William earnestly. 'I'm not going – not till they fetch me. Here! You begin. I don't want any. I've had lots of things. You eat it all.'

Her face radiant with anticipation, the little girl took up her spoon.

William leant back in a superior, benevolent manner and watched the smile freeze upon her face and her look of ecstasy change to one of fury. With a horrible suspicion at his heart he seized the spoon she had dropped and took a mouthful himself.

WILLIAM LEANT BACK IN A SUPERIOR, BENEVOLENT MANNER AND WATCHED THE SMILE FREEZE UPON HER FACE AND HER LOOK OF ECSTASY CHANGE TO ONE OF FURY.

He had brought the rice-mould by mistake!

CHAPTER 3

WILLIAM'S BURGLAR

When William first saw him he was leaning against the wall of the White Lion, gazing at the passers-by with a moody smile upon his villainous-looking countenance.

It was evident to any careful observer that he had not confined his attentions to the exterior of the White Lion.

William, at whose heels trotted his beloved mongrel (rightly named Jumble), was passing him with a casual glance, when something attracted his attention. He stopped and looked back, then, turning round, stood in front of the tall, untidy figure, gazing up at him with frank and unabashed curiosity.

'Who cut 'em off?' he said at last in an awed whisper.

The figure raised his hands and stroked the long hair down the side of his face.

'Now yer arskin',' he said with a grin.

'Well, who *did*?' persisted William.

'That 'ud be tellin',' answered his new friend, moving unsteadily from one foot to the other. 'See?'

'You got 'em cut off in the war,' said William firmly.

'I didn't. I bin in the wor orl right. Stroike me pink, I bin in the wor and *that's* the truth. But I didn't get 'em cut orf in the wor. Well, I'll stop kiddin' yer. I'll tell yer strite. I never 'ad none. *Nar!*'

William stood on tiptoe to peer under the untidy hair at the small apertures that in his strange new friend took the place of ears. Admiration shone in William's eyes.

'Was you *born* without 'em?' he said enviously.

His friend nodded.

'Nar don't yet go torkin' about it,' he went on modestly, though seeming to bask in the sun of William's evident awe and respect. 'I don't want all folks knowin' 'bout it. See? It kinder *marks* a man, this 'ere sort of thing. See? Makes 'im too easy to *track*, loike. That's why I grown me hair long. See? 'Ere, 'ave a drink?'

He put his head inside the window of the White Lion and roared out, 'Bottle o' lemonide fer the young gent.'

William followed him to a small table in the little sunny porch, and his heart swelled with pride as he sat and quaffed his beverage with a manly air. His friend, who said his name was Mr Blank, showed a most flattering interest in him. He elicited from him the whereabouts of his house and the number of his family, a description of the door and window fastenings, of the dining-room silver and his mother's jewellery.

William, his eyes fixed with a fascinated stare upon Mr Blank's ears, gave the required information readily, glad to be able in any way to interest this intriguing and mysterious being.

'Tell me about the war,' said William at last.

'It were orl right while it larsted,' said Mr Blank with a sigh. 'It were orl right, but I s'pose, like mos' things in this 'ere world, it couldn't larst fer ever. See?'

William set down the empty glass of lemonade and leant across the table, almost dizzy with the romance of the moment. Had Douglas, had Henry, had Ginger, had any of those boys who sat next him at school and joined in the feeble relaxations provided by the authorities out of school, ever done *this* – ever sat at a real table outside a real public-house drinking lemonade and talking to a man with no ears who'd fought in the war and who looked as if he might have done *anything?*

Jumble, meanwhile, sat and snapped at flies, frankly bored.

'Did you' – said William in a loud whisper – 'did you ever *kill* anyone?'

Mr Blank laughed a laugh that made William's blood curdle.

'DID YOU' – SAID WILLIAM IN A LOUD WHISPER – 'DID YOU
EVER KILL ANYONE?'

'Me kill anyone? Me kill anyone? '*Ondreds!*'

William breathed a sigh of satisfaction. Here was
romance and adventure incarnate.

'What do you do now the war's over?'

Mr Blank closed one eye.

'That 'ud be tellin', wudn't it?'

'I'll keep it awfully secret,' pleaded William. 'I'll never
tell anyone.'

Mr Blank shook his head.

'What yer want ter know fer, anyway?' he said.

William answered eagerly, his eyes alight.

''Cause I'd like to do jus' the same when I grow up.'

Mr Blank flung back his head and emitted guffaw after guffaw of unaffected mirth.

'Oh 'ell,' he said, wiping his eyes. 'Oh, stroike me pink! That's good, that is. You wait, young gent, you wait till you've growed up and see what yer pa says to it. Oh 'ell!'

He rose and pulled his cap down over his eyes.

'Well, I'll say good day to yer, young gent.'

William looked at him wistfully.

'I'd like to see you again, Mr Blank, I would, honest. Will you be here this afternoon?'

'Wot d'yer want to see me agine fer?' said Mr Blank suspiciously.

'I *like* you,' said William fervently. 'I like the way you talk, and I like the things you say, and I want to know about what you do!'

Mr Blank was obviously flattered.

'I may be round 'ere agine this arter, though I mike no promise. See? I've gotter be careful, I 'ave. I've gotter be careful 'oo sees me an' 'oo 'ears me, and where I go. That's the worst of 'aving no ears. See?'

William did not see, but he was thrilled to the soul by the mystery.

'An' you don't tell no one you seen me nor nothing abart me,' went on Mr Blank.

Pulling his cap still farther over his head, Mr Blank set off unsteadily down the road, leaving William to pay for his lemonade with his last penny.

He walked home, his heart set firmly on a lawless career of crime. Opposition he expected from his father and mother and Robert and Ethel, but his determination was fixed. He wondered if it would be very painful to have his ears cut off.

He entered the dining-room with an air of intense mystery, pulling his cap over his eyes, and looking round in a threatening manner.

'William, what *do* you mean by coming into the house in your cap? Take it off at once.'

William sighed. He wondered if Mr Blank had a mother.

When he returned he sat down and began quietly to remodel his life. He would not be an explorer, after all, nor an engine driver nor chimney sweep. He would be a man of mystery, a murderer, fighter, forger. He fingered his ears tentatively. They seemed fixed on jolly fast. He glanced with utter contempt at his father who had just come in. His father's life of blameless respectability seemed to him at that minute utterly despicable.

'The Wilkinsons over at Todfoot have had their house broken into now,' Mrs Brown was saying. '*All* her jewellery gone. They think it's a gang. It's just the villages round here. There seems to be one every day!'

William expressed his surprise.

'Oh, 'ell!' he ejaculated, with a slightly self-conscious air.

Mr Brown turned round and looked at his son.

'May I ask,' he said politely, 'where you picked up that expression?'

'I got it off one of my fren's,' said William with quiet pride.

'Then I'd take it as a personal favour,' went on Mr Brown, 'if you'd kindly refrain from airing your friends' vocabularies in this house.'

'He means you're never to say it again, William,' translated Mrs Brown sternly. '*Never.*'

'All right,' said William. 'I won't. See? I da— jolly well won't. Strike me pink. See?'

He departed with an air of scowling mystery and dignity combined, leaving his parents speechless with amazement.

That afternoon he returned to the White Lion. Mr

Blank was standing unobtrusively in the shadow of the wall.

''Ello, young gent,' he greeted William, 'nice dorg you've got.'

William looked proudly down at Jumble.

'You won't find,' he said proudly and with some truth, 'you won't find another dog like this — not for *miles*!'

'Will 'e be much good as a watchdog, now?' asked Mr Blank carelessly.

'Good?' said William, almost indignant at the question. 'There isn't any sort of dog he isn't good at!'

'Umph,' said Mr Blank, looking at him thoughtfully.

'Tell me about things you've *done*,' said William earnestly.

'Yus, I will, too,' said Mr Blank. 'But jus' you tell me first 'oo lives at all these 'ere nice 'ouses an' all about 'em. See?'

William readily complied, and the strange couple gradually wended their way along the road towards William's house. William stopped at the gate and considered deeply. He was torn between instincts of hospitality and a dim suspicion that his family would not afford to Mr Blank the courtesy which is a guest's due. He looked at Mr Blank's old green-black cap, long, untidy hair, dirty, lined, sly old face, muddy clothes and gaping boots, and decided quite finally that his mother would not allow him in her drawing-room.

'Will you,' he said tentatively, 'will you come roun' an' see our back garden? If we go behind these ole bushes and keep close along the wall, no one'll see us.'

To William's relief Mr Blank did not seem to resent the

WILLIAM DEPARTED WITH AN AIR OF SCOWLING MYSTERY, LEAVING HIS PARENTS SPEECHLESS WITH AMAZEMENT.

suggestion of secrecy. They crept along the wall in silence except for Jumble, who loudly worried Mr Blank's trailing boot strings as he walked. They reached a part of the back garden that was not visible from the house and sat down together under a shady tree.

'P'raps,' began Mr Blank politely, 'you could bring a bit o' tea out to me on the quiet like.'

'I'll ask Mother—' began William.

'Oh no,' said Mr Blank modestly. 'I don't want ter give no one no trouble. Just a slice o' bread, if you can find it, without troublin' no one. See?'

William had a brilliant idea.

'Let's go 'cross to that window an' get in,' he said eagerly. 'That's the lib'ry and no one uses it 'cept Father, and he's not in till later.'

Mr Blank insisted on tying Jumble up, then he swung himself dexterously through the window. William gave a gasp of admiration.

'You did that fine,' he said.

Again Mr Blank closed one eye.

'Not the first time I've got in at a winder, young gent, nor the larst, I bet. Not by a long way. See?'

William followed more slowly. His eyes gleamed with pride. This hero of romance and adventure was now his guest, under his roof.

'Make yourself quite at home, Mr Blank,' he said with an air of intense politeness.

Mr Blank did. He emptied Mr Brown's cigar box into his pocket. He drank three glasses of Mr Brown's whiskey and soda. While William's back was turned he filled his

MR BLANK MADE HIMSELF QUITE AT HOME.

pockets with the silver ornaments from the mantelpiece. He began to inspect the drawers in Mr Brown's desk. Then:

'William! Come to tea!'

'You stay here,' whispered William. 'I'll bring you some.'

But luck was against him. It was a visitor's tea in the drawing-room, and Mrs de Vere Carter, a neighbour, there, in all her glory. She rose from her seat with an ecstatic murmur.

'Willie! *Dear* child! *Sweet* little soul!'

With one arm she crushed the infuriated William against her belt, with the other she caressed his hair. Then William in moody silence sat down in a corner and began to eat bread and butter. Every time he prepared to slip a piece into his pocket, he found his mother's or Mrs de Vere Carter's eyes fixed upon him and hastily began to eat it himself. He sat, miserable and hot, seeing only the heroic figure starving in the next room, and planned a raid on the larder as soon as he could reasonably depart. Every now and then he scowled across at Mrs de Vere Carter and made a movement with his hands as though pulling a cap over his eyes. He invested even his eating with an air of dark mystery.

Then Robert, his elder brother, came in, followed by a

thin, pale man with eyeglasses and long hair.

'This is Mr Lewes, Mother,' said Robert with an air of pride and triumph. 'He's editor of *Fiddle Strings*.'

There was an immediate stir and sensation. Robert had often talked of his famous friend. In fact Robert's family was weary of the sound of his name, but this was the first time Robert had induced him to leave the haunts of his genius to visit the Brown household.

Mr Lewes bowed with a set, stern, self-conscious expression, as though to convey to all that his celebrity was more of a weight than a pleasure to him. Mrs de Vere Carter bridled and fluttered, for *Fiddle Strings* had a society column and a page of scrappy 'News of the Town', and Mrs de Vere Carter's greatest ambition was to see her name in print.

Mr Lewes sat back in his chair, took his teacup as though it were a fresh addition to his responsibilities, and began to talk. He talked apparently without even breathing. He began on the weather, drifted on to art and music, and was just beginning a monologue on The Novel, when William rose and crept from the room like a guilty spirit. He found Mr Blank under the library table, having heard a noise in the kitchen and fearing a visitor. A cigar and a silver snuffer had fallen from his pocket to the floor. He hastily replaced them. William went up and took another look at the wonderful ears and heaved a sigh of relief. While parted from his strange friend he had a horrible suspicion that the whole thing was a dream.

'I'll go to the larder and get you sumthin',' he said. 'You jus' stay there.'

'I think, young gent,' said Mr Blank, 'I think I'll just go an' look round upstairs on the quiet like, an' you needn't mention it to no one. See?'

Again he performed the fascinating wink.

They crept on tiptoe into the hall, but – the drawing-room door was ajar.

'William!'

William's heart stood still. He could hear his mother coming across the room, then – she stood in the doorway. Her face filled with horror as her eyes fell upon Mr Blank.

'*William!*' she said.

William's feelings were beyond description. Desperately he sought for an explanation for his friend's presence. With what pride and sangfroid had Robert announced his uninvited guest! William determined to try it, at any rate. He advanced boldly into the drawing-room.

'This is Mr Blank, Mother,' he announced jauntily. 'He hasn't got no ears.'

Mr Blank stood in the background, awaiting developments. Flight was now impossible.

The announcement fell flat. There was nothing but horror upon the five silent faces that confronted William. He made a last desperate effort.

'He's bin in the war,' he pleaded. 'He's – killed folks.'

Then the unexpected happened.

Mrs de Vere Carter rose with a smile of welcome. In her mind's eye she saw the touching story already in print – tattered hero – the gracious lady – the age of Democracy. The stage was laid and that dark, pale young man had only to watch and listen.

'Ah, one of our dear heroes! My poor, brave man! A cup of tea, my dear,' turning to William's thunderstruck mother. 'And he may sit down, may he not?' She kept her face well turned towards the sardonic-looking Mr Lewes. He must not miss a word or gesture. 'How *proud* we are to do anything for our dear heroes! Wounded, perhaps? Ah, poor man!' She floated across to him with a cup of tea and plied him with bread and butter and cake. William sat down meekly on a chair, looking rather pale. Mr Blank, whose philosophy was to take the goods the gods gave and not look to the future, began to make a hearty meal. 'Are you looking for work, my poor man?' asked Mrs de Vere Carter, leaning forward in her chair.

Her poor man replied with simple, manly directness

that he 'was dam'd if he was. See?' Mr Lewes began to discuss The Drama with Robert. Mrs de Vere Carter raised her voice.

'*How* you must have suffered! Yes, there is suffering ingrained in your face. A piece of shrapnel? Ten inches square? Right in at one hip and out at the other? Oh, my poor man! *How* I feel for you. How all class distinctions vanish at such a time. How—'

She stopped while Mr Blank drank his tea. In fact, all conversation ceased while Mr Blank drank his tea, just as conversation on a station ceases while a train passes through.

Mrs Brown looked helplessly around her. When Mr Blank had eaten a plate of sandwiches, a plate of bread and butter, and half a cake, he rose slowly, keeping one hand over the pocket in which reposed the silver ornaments.

'Well 'm,' he said, touching his cap. 'Thank you kindly. I've 'ad a fine tea. I 'ave. A dam' fine tea. An' I'll not forget yer kindness to a pore ole soldier.' Here he winked brazenly at William. 'An' good day ter you orl.'

Mrs de Vere Carter floated out to the front door with him, and William followed as in a dream.

Mrs Brown found her voice.

'We'd better have the chair disinfected,' she murmured to Ethel.

Then Mrs de Vere Carter returned smiling to herself and eyeing the young editor surmisingly.

'I witnessed a pretty scene the other day in a suburban drawing-room . . .' It might begin like that.

William followed the amazing figure round the house

'ARE YOU LOOKING FOR WORK, MY POOR MAN?' ASKED
MRS DE VERE CARTER.

59

again to the library window. Here it turned to him with a friendly grin.

'I'm just goin' to 'ave that look round upstairs now. See?' he said. 'An' once more, yer don't need ter say nothin' to no one. See?'

With the familiar, beloved gesture he drew his old cap down over his eyes, and was gone.

William wandered upstairs a few minutes later to find his visitor standing at the landing window, his pockets bulging.

'I'm goin' to try this 'ere window, young gent,' he said in a quick, business-like voice. 'I see yer pa coming in at the front gate. Give me a shove. Quick, nar.'

Mr Brown entered the drawing-room.

'Mulroyd's had his house burgled now,' he said. 'Every bit of his wife's jewellery gone. They've got some clues, though. It's a gang all right, and one of them is a chap without ears. Grows his hair long to hide it. But it's a clue. The police are hunting for him.'

He looked in amazement at the horror-stricken faces before him. Mrs Brown sat down weakly.

'Ethel, my smelling salts! They're on the mantelpiece.'

Robert grew pale.

'Good Lord – my silver cricket cup,' he gasped, racing upstairs.

The landing window had been too small, and Mr Blank too big, though William did his best.

There came to the astounded listeners the sound of a fierce scuffle, then Robert descended, his hair rumpled and his tie awry, holding William by the arm. William looked pale and apprehensive. 'He was there,' panted Robert, 'just getting out of the window. He chucked the things out of his pockets and got away. I couldn't stop him. And – and William was there—'

William's face assumed the expression of one who is prepared for the worst.

'The plucky little chap! Struggling with him! Trying to pull him back from the window! All by himself!'

'I *wasn't*,' cried William excitedly. 'I was *helping* him. He's my *friend*. I—'

But they heard not a word. They crowded round him, praised him, shook hands with him, asked if he was hurt. Mrs de Vere Carter kept up one perpetual scream of delight and congratulation.

'The *dear* boy! The little *pet*! How *brave*! What *courage*! What an *example* to us all! And the horrid, wretched man! Posing as a *hero*. Wangling himself into the sweet child's confidence. Are you hurt, my precious? Did the nasty man hurt you? You *darling* boy!'

When the babel had somewhat subsided, Mr Brown

came forward and laid a hand on William's shoulder.

'I'm very pleased with you, my boy,' he said. 'You can buy anything you like tomorrow up to five shillings.'

William's bewildered countenance cleared.

'Thank you, Father,' he said meekly.

CHAPTER 4

THE KNIGHT AT ARMS

'A knight,' said Miss Drew, who was struggling to inspire her class with enthusiasm for Tennyson's 'Idylls of the King', 'a knight was a person who spent his time going round succouring the oppressed.'

'Suckin' wot?' said William, bewildered.

'Succour means to help. He spent his time helping anyone who was in trouble.'

'How much did he get for it?' asked William.

'Nothing, of course,' said Miss Drew, appalled by the base commercialism of the twentieth century. 'He helped the poor because he *loved* them, William. He had a lot of adventures and fighting and he helped beautiful, persecuted damsels.'

William's respect for the knight rose.

'Of course,' said Miss Drew hastily, 'they needn't necessarily be beautiful, but, in most of the stories we have, they were beautiful.'

There followed some stories of fighting and adventure and the rescuing of beautiful damsels. The idea of the thing began to take hold of William's imagination.

'I say,' he said to his chum Ginger after school, 'that knight thing sounds all right. Suckin' – I mean helpin' people an' fightin' an' all that. I wun't mind doin' it an' you could be my squire.'

'Yes,' said Ginger slowly, 'I'd thought of doin' it, but I'd thought of *you* bein' the squire.'

'Well,' said William after a pause, 'let's be squires in turn. You first,' he added hastily.

'Wot'll you give me if I'm first?' said Ginger, displaying again the base commercialism of the age.

William considered.

'I'll give you first drink out of a bottle of ginger ale wot I'm goin' to get with my next money. It'll be three weeks off 'cause they're takin' the next two weeks to pay for an ole window wot my ball slipped into by mistake.'

He spoke with the bitterness that always characterised his statements of the injustice of the grown-up world.

'All right,' said Ginger.

'I won't forget about the drink of ginger ale.'

'No, you won't,' said Ginger simply. 'I'll remind you all right. Well, let's set off.'

''Course,' said William, 'it would be *nicer* with armour an' horses an' trumpets, but I 'spect folks 'ud think anyone a bit soft wot went about in the streets in armour now, 'cause these times is different. She said so. Anyway, she said we could still be knights an' help people, di'n't she? Anyway, I'll get my bugle. That'll be *something*.'

William's bugle had just returned to public life after one of its periodic terms of retirement into his father's keeping.

William took his bugle proudly in one hand and his pistol (the glorious result of a dip in the bran tub at a school party) in the other, and, sternly denying themselves the pleasures of afternoon school, off the two set upon the road of romance and adventure.

'I'll carry the bugle,' said Ginger, ' 'cause I'm squire.'

William was loath to give up his treasure.

'Well, I'll carry it now,' he said, 'but when I begin fightin' folks, I'll give it you to hold.'

They walked along for about a mile without meeting anyone. William began to be aware of a sinking feeling in the region of his waist.

'I wonder wot they *eat*,' he said at last. 'I'm gettin' so's I wouldn't mind sumthin' to eat.'

'We di'n't ought to have set off before dinner,' said the squire with after-the-event wisdom. 'We ought to have waited till *after* dinner.'

'You ought to have *brought* sumthin',' said William severely. 'You're the squire. You're not much of a squire not to have brought sumthin' for me to eat.'

'An' me,' put in Ginger. 'If I'd brought any I'd have brought it for me more'n for you.'

William fingered his minute pistol.

'If we meet any wild animals . . .' he said darkly.

A cow gazed at them mournfully over a hedge.

'You might go an' milk that,' suggested William. 'Milk 'ud be better'n nothing.'

'*You* go an' milk it.'

'No, I'm not squire. I bet squires did the milkin'. Knights wun't of done the milkin'.'

'I'll remember,' said Ginger bitterly, 'when you're squire, all the things wot you said a squire ought to do when I was squire.'

They entered the field and gazed at the cow from a respectful distance. She turned her eyes upon them sadly.

'Go on!' said the knight to his reluctant squire.

'I'm not good at cows,' objected that gentleman.

'Well, I will, then!' said William with reckless bravado, and advanced boldly upon the animal. The animal very slightly lowered its horns (perhaps in sign of greeting) and emitted a sonorous mo-o-o-o-o. Like lightning the gallant pair made for the road.

'Anyway,' said William gloomily, 'we'd got nothin' to put it in, so we'd only of got tossed for nothin', p'raps, if we'd gone on.'

They walked on down the road till they came to a pair of iron gates and a drive that led up to a big house. William's spirits rose. His hunger was forgotten.

'Come on!' he said. 'We might find someone to rescue here. It looks like a place where there might be someone to rescue.'

There was no one in the garden to question the right of entry of two small boys armed with a bugle and a toy pistol. Unchallenged they went up to the house. While the knight was wondering whether to blow his bugle at the front door or by the open window, they caught sight suddenly of a vision inside the window. It was a girl as fair and slim and beautiful as any wandering knight could desire. And she was speaking fast and passionately.

William, ready for all contingencies, marshalled his forces.

'Follow me!' he whispered and crept on all fours nearer the window. They could see a man now, an elderly man with white hair and a white beard.

'And how long will you keep me in this vile prison,' she was saying in a voice that trembled with anger, 'base wretch that you are?'

'Crumbs!' ejaculated William.

'Ha! Ha!' sneered the man. 'I have you in my power. I will keep you here a prisoner till you sign the paper which will make me master of all your wealth, and beware, girl, if you do not sign, you may answer for it with your life!'

'Golly!' murmured William.

Then he crawled away into the bushes, followed by his attendant squire.

'Well,' said William, his face purple with excitement, 'we've found someone to rescue all *right*. He's a base wretch, wot she said, all *right*.'

'Will you kill him?' said the awed squire.

'How big was he? Could you see?' said William the discreet.

'He was ever so big. Great big face he had, too, with a beard.'

'Then I won't try killin' him – not straight off. I'll think of some plan – somethin' cunnin'.'

He sat with his chin on his hands, gazing into space, till they were surprised by the opening of the front door and the appearance of a tall, thick-set, elderly man. William quivered with excitement. The man went along a path through the bushes. William and Ginger followed on all fours with elaborate caution. At every almost inaudible sound from Ginger, William turned his red, frowning face on to him with a resounding 'Shh!' The path ended at a small shed with a locked door. The man opened the door – the key stood in the lock – and entered.

Promptly William, with a snarl expressive of cunning and triumph, hurled himself at the door and turned the key in the lock.

'Here!' came an angry shout from inside. 'Who's that? What the devil—'

'You low ole caitiff!' said William through the keyhole.

'Who the deuce—' exploded the voice.

'You base wretch, like wot she said you was,' bawled William, his mouth still applied closely to the keyhole.

WILLIAM AND GINGER FOLLOWED ON ALL FOURS WITH
ELABORATE CAUTION.

'Let me out at once, or I'll—'

'You mean ole oppressor!'

'Who the deuce are you? What's the tomfool trick? Let me *out*! Do you hear?'

A resounding kick shook the door.

'I've gotter pistol,' said William sternly. 'I'll shoot you dead if you kick the door down, you mangy ole beast!'

The sound of kicking ceased and a scrambling and scraping, accompanied by oaths, proceeded from the interior.

'I'll stay on guard,' said William with the tense expression of the soldier at his post, 'an' you go an' set her free. Go an' blow the bugle at the front door, then they'll know something's happened,' he added simply.

Miss Priscilla Greene was pouring out tea in the drawing-room. Two young men and a maiden were the recipients of her hospitality.

'Dad will be here in a minute,' she said. 'He's just gone to the darkroom to see to some photos he'd left in toning or fixing, or something. We'll get on with the rehearsal as soon as he comes. We'd just rehearsed the scene he and I have together, so we're ready for the ones where we all come in.'

'How did it go off?'

'Oh, quite well. We knew our parts, anyway.'

'I think the village will enjoy it.'

'Anyway, it's never very critical, is it? And it loves a melodrama.'

'Yes. I wonder if Father knows you're here. He said he'd come straight back. Perhaps I'd better go and find him.'

'Oh, let me go, Miss Greene,' said one of the youths ardently.

'Well, I'd don't know whether you'd find the place. It's a shed in the garden that he uses. We use it half as a dark-room and half as a coal-cellar.'

'I'll go—'

He stopped. A nightmare sound, as discordant as it was ear-splitting, filled the room. Miss Greene sank back into her chair, suddenly white. One of the young men let a cup of tea fall neatly from his fingers on to the floor and there crash into fragments. The young lady visitor emitted a scream that would have done credit to a factory siren. Then at the open French window appeared a small boy holding a bugle, purple-faced with the effort of his performance.

One of the young men was the first to recover speech. He stepped away from the broken crockery on the floor as if to disclaim all responsibility for it and said sternly:

'Did you make that horrible noise?'

Miss Greene began to laugh hysterically.

'Do have some tea now you've come,' she said to Ginger.

Ginger remembered the pangs of hunger, of which excitement had momentarily rendered him oblivious, and, deciding that there was no time like the present, took a cake from the stand and began to consume it in silence.

'You'd better be careful,' said the young lady to her hostess; 'he might have escaped from the asylum. He looks mad. He had a very mad look, I thought, when he was standing at the window.'

'He's evidently hungry, anyway. I can't think why Father doesn't come.'

Here Ginger, fortified by a walnut bun, remembered his mission.

'It's all right now,' he said. 'You can go home. He's shut up. Me an' William shut him up.'

'You see!' said the young lady, with a meaning glance around. 'I *said* he was from the asylum. He looked mad. We'd better humour him and ring up the asylum. Have another cake, darling boy,' she said in a tone of honeyed sweetness.

Nothing loath, Ginger selected an ornate pyramid of icing.

At this point there came a bellowing and crashing and tramping outside and Miss Priscilla's father, roaring fury and threats of vengeance, hurled himself into the room. Miss Priscilla's father had made his escape by a small window at the other end of the shed. To do this he had had to climb over the coals in the dark. His face and hands and clothes and once-white beard were covered with coal. His eyes gleamed whitely.

'An abominable attack . . . utterly unprovoked . . . dastardly ruffians!'

Here he stopped to splutter because his mouth was full of coal dust. While he was spluttering, William, who had just discovered that his bird had flown, appeared at the window.

'He's got out,' he said reproachfully. 'Look at him. He's got out. An' all our trouble for nothing. Why di'n't someone *stop* him gettin' out?'

William and Ginger sat on the railing that separated their houses.

'It's not really much *fun* bein' a knight,' said William slowly.

'No,' agreed Ginger. 'You never know when folks *is* oppressed. An' anyway, wot's one afternoon away from school to make such a fuss about?'

'HE'S GOT OUT,' WILLIAM SAID REPROACHFULLY. 'WHY
DI'N'T SOMEONE STOP HIM GETTIN' OUT?'

'Seems to me from wot Father said,' went on William
gloomily, 'you'll have to wait a jolly long time for that
drink of ginger ale.'

An expression of dejection came over Ginger's face.

'An' you wasn't even ever squire,' he said. Then he
brightened.

'They were jolly good cakes, wasn't they?' he said.

William's lips curved into a smile of blissful reminis-
cence.

'*Jolly* good!' he agreed.

CHAPTER 5

WILLIAM'S HOBBY

Uncle George was William's godfather, and he was intensely interested in William's upbringing. It was an interest with which William would gladly have dispensed. Uncle George's annual visit was to William a purgatory only to be endured by a resolutely philosophic attitude of mind and the knowledge that sooner or later it must come to an end. Uncle George had an ideal of what a boy should be, and it was a continual grief to him that William fell so short of this ideal. But he never relinquished his efforts to make William conform to it.

His ideal was a gentle boy of exquisite courtesy and of intellectual pursuits. Such a boy he could have loved. It was hard that fate had endowed him with a godson like William. William was neither quiet nor gentle, nor courteous nor intellectual – but William was intensely human.

The length of Uncle George's visit this year was beginning to reach the limits of William's patience. He was beginning to feel that sooner or later something must happen. For five weeks now he had (reluctantly) accompanied Uncle George upon his morning walk, he had (generally unsuccessfully) tried to maintain that state of absolute quiet that Uncle George's afternoon rest required, he had in the evening listened wearily to Uncle George's stories of his youth. His usual feeling of mild contempt for Uncle George was beginning to give way to one which was much stronger.

'Now, William,' said Uncle George at breakfast, 'I'm afraid it's going to rain today, so we'll do a little work together this morning, shall we? Nothing like work, is there? Your Arithmetic's a bit shaky, isn't it? We'll rub that up. We *love* our work, don't we?'

William eyed him coldly.

'I don't think I'd better get muddlin' up my school work,' he said. 'I shouldn't like to be more on than the other boys next term. It wouldn't be fair to them.'

Uncle George rubbed his hands.

'That feeling does you credit, my boy,' he said, 'but if we go over some of the old work, no harm can be done. History, now. There's nothing like History, is there?'

William agreed quite heartily that there wasn't.

'We'll do some History, then,' said Uncle George briskly. 'The lives of the great. Most inspiring. Better than those terrible things you used to waste your time on, eh?'

The 'terrible things' had included a trumpet, a beloved

motor hooter, and an ingenious instrument very dear to William's soul that reproduced most realistically the sound of two cats fighting. These, at Uncle George's request, had been confiscated by William's father. Uncle George had not considered them educational. They also disturbed his afternoon rest.

Uncle George settled himself and William down for a nice quiet morning in the library. William, looking round for escape, found none. The outside world was wholly uninviting. The rain came down in torrents. Moreover, the five preceding weeks had broken William's spirits. He realised the impossibility of evading Uncle George. His own family were not sympathetic. They suffered from him considerably during the rest of the year and were not sorry to see him absorbed completely by Uncle George's conscientious zeal.

So Uncle George seated himself slowly and ponderously in an armchair by the fire.

'When I was a boy, William,' he began, leaning back and joining the tips of his fingers together, 'I loved my studies. I'm sure you love your studies, don't you? Which do you love most?'

'Me?' said William. 'I like shootin' and playin' Red Injuns.'

'Yes, yes,' said Uncle George impatiently, 'but those

aren't *studies*, William. You must aim at being *gentle*.'

'It's not much good bein' *gentle* when you're playin' Red Injuns,' said William stoutly. 'A *gentle* Red Injun wun't get much done.'

'Ah, but why play Red Indians?' said Uncle George. 'A nasty rough game. No, we'll talk about History. You must mould your character upon that of the great heroes, William. You must be a Clive, a Napoleon, a Wolfe.'

'I've often been a wolf,' said William. 'That game's nearly as good as Red Injuns. An' Bears is a good game too. We might have Bears here,' he went on brightening. 'Jus' you an' me. Would you sooner be bear or hunter? I'd sooner be hunter,' he hinted gently.

'You misunderstand,' said Uncle George. 'I mean Wolfe the man, Wolfe the hero.'

William, who had little patience with heroes who came within the school curriculum, relapsed into gloom.

'What lessons do we learn from such names, my boy?' went on Uncle George.

William was on the floor behind Uncle George's chair endeavouring to turn a somersault in a very restricted space.

'History lessons an' dates an' things,' he said shortly. 'An' the things they 'spect you to remember—' he added with disgust.

'No, no,' said Uncle George, but the fire was hot and his chair was comfortable and his educational zeal was dying away, 'to endure the buffets of fate with equanimity, to smile at misfortune, to endure whatever comes, and so on—'

He stopped suddenly.

WILLIAM WAS ON THE FLOOR BEHIND UNCLE GEORGE'S CHAIR ENDEAVOURING TO TURN A SOMERSAULT IN A VERY RESTRICTED SPACE.

William had managed the somersault, but it had somehow brought his feet into collision with Uncle George's neck. Uncle George sleepily shifted his position.

'Boisterous! Boisterous!' he murmured disapprovingly. 'You should combine the gentleness of a Moore with the courage of a Wellington, William.'

William now perceived that Uncle George's eyelids were drooping slowly and William's sudden statuesque calm would have surprised many of his instructors.

The silence and the warmth of the room had their effect. In less than three minutes Uncle George was dead to the world around him.

William's form relaxed, then he crept up to look closely at the face of his enemy. He decided that he disliked it intensely. Something must be done at once. He looked round the room. There were not many weapons handy. Only his mother's workbox stood on a chair by the window, and on it a pile of socks belonging to Robert, William's elder brother. Beneath either arm of his chair one of Uncle George's coat-tails protruded. William soon departed on his way rejoicing, while on to one of Uncle George's coat-tails was firmly stitched a bright blue sock and on to the other a brilliant orange one. Robert's taste in socks was decidedly loud. William felt almost happy. The rain had stopped and he spent the morning with some of his friends whom he met in the road. They went bear-hunting in the wood; and though no bears were found, still their disappointment was considerably allayed by the fact that one of them saw a mouse and another one distinctly smelt a rabbit. William returned to lunch whistling to himself and had the intense satisfaction of seeing Uncle George enter the dining-room, obviously roused from his slumbers by the luncheon bell, and obviously quite unaware of the blue and orange socks that still adorned his person.

'Curious!' he ejaculated, as Ethel, William's grown-up sister, pointed out the blue sock to him. 'Most curious!'

William departed discreetly, muttering something about 'better tidy up a bit', which drew from his sister expressions of surprise and solicitous questions as to his state of health.

'Most curious!' said Uncle George again, who had now discovered the orange sock.

When William returned, all excitement was over and Uncle George was consuming roast beef with energy.

'Ah, William,' he said, 'we must complete the History lesson soon. Nothing like History. Nothing like History. Nothing like History. Teaches us to endure the buffets of fate with equanimity and to smile at misfortune. Then we must do some Geography.' William groaned. 'Most fascinating study. Rivers, mountains, cities, etc. Most improving. The morning should be devoted to intellectual work at your age, William, and the afternoon to the quiet pursuit of – some improving hobby. You would then find the true joy of life.'

To judge from William's countenance he did not wholly agree, but he made no objection. He had learnt that objection was useless, and against Uncle George's eloquence silence was his only weapon.

After lunch Uncle George followed his usual custom and retired to rest. William went to the shed in the back garden and continued the erection of a rabbit hutch that he had begun a few days before. He hoped that if he made a hutch, Providence would supply a rabbit. He whistled blithely as he knocked nails in at random.

'William, you mustn't do that now.'

He turned a stern gaze upon his mother.

'Why not?' he said.

'Uncle George is resting.'

With a crushing glance at her he strolled away from the shed. Someone had left the lawn mower in the middle of the lawn. With one of his rare impulses of pure virtue he determined to be useful. Also, he rather liked mowing the grass.

'William, don't do that now,' called his sister from the

window. 'Uncle George is resting.'

He deliberately drove the mowing machine into the middle of the garden bed and left it there. He was beginning to feel desperate. Then:

'What *can* I do?' he said bitterly to Ethel, who was still at the window.

'You'd better find some quiet, improving hobby,' she said unkindly as she went away.

It is a proof of the utterly broken state of William's spirit that he did actually begin to think of hobbies, but none of those that occurred to him interested him. Stamp-collecting, pressed flowers, crest-collecting – Ugh!

He set off down the road, his hands in his pockets and his brows drawn into a stern frown. He amused himself by imagining Uncle George in various predicaments, lost on a desert island, captured by pirates, or carried off by an eagle. Then something in the window of a house he passed caught his eye and he stopped suddenly. It was a stuffed bird under a glass case. Now that was something *like* a hobby, stuffing dead animals! He wouldn't mind having that for a hobby. And it was quite quiet. He could do it while Uncle George was resting. And it must be quite easy. The first thing to do of course was to find a dead animal. Any old thing would do to begin on. A dead cat or dog. He would do bigger ones like bears and lions later on. He spent nearly an hour in a fruitless search for a dead cat or dog. He searched the ditches on both sides of the road and several gardens. He began to have a distinct sense of grievance against the race of cats and dogs in general for not dying in his vicinity. At the end of the hour he found a small dead frog. It was very dry and shrivelled, but it was certainly a *dead* frog and would do to begin on. He took it home in his pocket. He wondered what they did first in stuffing dead animals. He'd heard something about 'tannin'' them. But what was 'tannin',' and how did one get it? Then he remembered suddenly having heard Ethel talk about the 'tannin'' in tea. So *that* was all right. The first thing to do was to get some tea. He went to the drawing-room. It was empty, but upon the table near the fire was a tea tray and two cups. Evidently his mother and sister had just had tea there. He put the frog at the bottom of a cup and carefully filled the cup with tea from the teapot. Then he left it to soak and went out into the garden.

A few minutes later William's mother entered the drawing-room.

Uncle George had finished resting and was standing by the mantelpiece with a cup in his hand.

'I see you poured out my tea for me,' he said. 'But rather a curious taste. Doubtless you boil the milk now.

Safer, of course. Much safer. But it imparts a curious flavour.'

He took another sip.

'But – I didn't pour out your tea—' began Mrs Brown. Here William entered. He looked quickly at the table.

'Who's meddlin' with my frog?' he said angrily. 'It's my hobby, an' I'm stuffin' frogs an' someone's been an' took my frog. I left it on the table.'

'On the table?' said his mother.

'Yes. In a cup of tea. Gettin' tannin'. You know. For stuffin'. I was puttin' him in tannin' first. I—'

Uncle George grew pale. In frozen silence he put a spoon into his cup and investigated the contents. In still more frozen silence Mrs Brown and William watched. That moment held all the cumulative horror of a Greek tragedy. Then Uncle George put down his cup and went silently from the room. On his face was the expression of one who is going to look up the first train home. Fate had sent him a buffet he could not endure with equanimity, a misfortune at which he could not smile, and Fate had avenged William for much.

IN FROZEN SILENCE UNCLE GEORGE PUT A SPOON INTO HIS
CUP AND INVESTIGATED THE CONTENTS. IN STILL MORE
FROZEN SILENCE MRS BROWN AND WILLIAM WATCHED.

CHAPTER 6

THE RIVALS

William was aware of a vague feeling of apprehension when he heard that Joan Clive, the little girl who lived next door, was having a strange cousin to stay for three weeks. All his life, William had accepted Joan's adoration and homage with condescending indifference, but he did not like to imagine a possible rival.

'What's he *coming* for?' he demanded with an ungracious scowl, perched uncomfortably and dangerously on the high wall that separated the two gardens and glaring down at Joan. 'What's he comin' *for*, anyway?'

''Cause mother's invited him,' explained Joan simply, with a shake of her dark curls. 'He's called Cuthbert. She says he's a sweet little boy.'

'*Sweet!*' echoed William in a tone of exaggerated horror. 'Ugh!'

'Well,' said Joan, with the smallest note of indignation in her voice, 'you needn't play with him if you don't like.'

'*Me?* Play? With *him?*' scowled William as if he could not believe his ears. 'I'm not likely to go playin' with a kid like wot *he'll* be!'

Joan raised aggrieved blue eyes.

'You're a *horrid* boy sometimes, William!' she said. 'Anyway, I shall have him to play with soon.'

It was the first time he had received anything but admiration from her.

He scowled speechlessly.

Cuthbert arrived the next morning.

William was restless and ill at ease, and several times climbed the ladder for a glimpse of the guest, but all he could see was the garden inhabited only by a cat and a gardener. He amused himself by throwing stones at the cat till he hit the gardener by mistake and then fled precipitately before a storm of abuse. William and the gardener were enemies of very long standing. After dinner he went out again into the garden and stood gazing through a chink in the wall.

Cuthbert was in the garden.

Though as old and as tall as William, he was dressed in an embroidered tunic, very short knickers, and white socks. Over his blue eyes his curls were brushed up into a golden halo.

He was a picturesque child.

'What shall we do?' Joan was saying. 'Would you like to play hide and seek?'

'No; leth not play at rough gameth,' said Cuthbert.

With a wild spasm of joy William realised that his enemy lisped. It is always well to have a handle against one's enemies.

'What shall we do, then?' said Joan, somewhat wearily.

'Leth thit down an' I'll tell you fairy thorieth,' said Cuthbert.

A loud snort from inside the wall just by his ear startled him, and he clutched Joan's arm.

'What'th that?' he said.

There were sounds of clambering feet on the other side of the wall, then William's grimy countenance appeared.

'Hello, Joan!' he said, ignoring the stranger.

Joan's eyes brightened.

'Come and play with us, William,' she begged.

'We don't want dirty little boyth,' murmured Cuthbert fastidiously. William could not, with justice, have objected to the epithet. He had spent the last half-hour climbing on to the rafters of the disused coach house, and dust and cobwebs adorned his face and hair.

'He's *always* like that,' explained Joan carelessly.

By this time William had thought of a suitable rejoinder.

'All right,' he jeered, 'don't look at me then. Go on tellin' fairy *thorieth*.'

Cuthbert flushed angrily.

'You're a nathty rude little boy,' he said. 'I'll tell my mother.'

Thus war was declared.

He came to tea the next day. Not all William's pleading could persuade his mother to cancel the invitation.

'Well,' said William darkly, 'wait till you've *seen* him, that's all. Wait till you've heard him *speakin'*. He can't talk even. He can't *play*. He tells fairy stories. He don't like *dirt*. He's got long hair an' a funny long coat. He's *awful*, I tell you. I don't *want* to have him to tea. I don't want to be washed an' all just because *he's* comin' to tea.'

But as usual William's eloquence availed nothing.

Several people came to tea that afternoon, and there was a sudden silence when Mrs Clive, Joan and Cuthbert entered. Cuthbert was in a white silk tunic embroidered with blue, he wore white shoes and white silk socks. His golden curls shone. He looked angelic.

'Oh, the darling!'

'Isn't he adorable?'

'What a *picture*!'

'Come here, sweetheart.'

Cuthbert was quite used to this sort of thing.

They were more delighted than ever with him when they discovered his lisp.

His manners were perfect. He raised his face, with a charming smile, to be kissed, then sat down on the sofa between Joan and Mrs Clive, swinging long bare legs.

William, sitting, an unwilling victim, on a small chair in a corner of the room, brushed and washed till he shone again, was conscious of a feeling of fury quite apart from the usual sense of outrage that he always felt upon such an occasion. It was bad enough to be washed till the soap went into his eyes and down his ears despite all his protests. It was bad enough to have had his hair brushed till his head smarted. It was bad enough to be hustled out of his comfortable jersey into his Eton suit which he loathed. But to see Joan, *his* Joan, sitting next to the strange, dressed-up, lisping boy, smiling and talking to him, that was almost more than he could bear with calmness. Previously, as has been said, he had received Joan's adoration with coldness, but previously there had been no rival.

'William,' said his mother, 'take Joan and Cuthbert and show them your engine and books and things. Remember you're the *host*, dear,' she murmured as he passed. 'Try to make them happy.'

He turned upon her a glance that would have made a stronger woman quail.

Silently he led them up to his play room.

'There's my engine, an' my books. You can play with them,' he said coldly to Cuthbert. 'Let's go and play in the garden, you and me, Joan.'

But Joan shook her head.

'I don't thuppoth the'd care to go out without me,' said Cuthbert airily. '*I'll* go with you. Thith boy can play here if he liketh.'

And William, artist in vituperation as he was, could think of no response.

He followed them into the garden, and there came upon him a wild determination to show his superiority.

'You can't climb that tree,' he began.

'I can,' said Cuthbert sweetly.

'Well, *climb* it then,' he said grimly.

'No, I don't want to get my thingth all methed. I *can* climb, but you can't. He can't climb it, Joan, he'th trying to pretend he can climb it when he can't. He knowth I can climb it, but I don't want to get my thingth methed.'

Joan smiled admiringly at Cuthbert.

'I'll *show* you,' said William desperately. 'I'll just *show* you.'

He showed them.

He climbed till the treetop swayed with his weight, then descended, hot and triumphant. The tree was covered with green lichen, a great part of which had deposited itself upon William's suit. His efforts had also twisted his collar round till its stud was beneath his ear. His heated countenance beamed with pride.

For a moment Cuthbert was nonplussed. Then he said scornfully:

'Don't he look a *fright*, Joan?'

Joan giggled.

But William was wholly engrossed in his self-imposed task of 'showing them'. He led them to the bottom of the garden, where a small stream (now almost dry) disappeared into a narrow tunnel to flow under the road and reappear in the field at the other side.

'You can't crawl through that,' challenged William, 'you can't *do* it. I've *done* it, done it often. I bet *you* can't. I bet you can't get halfway. I—'

'Well, *do* it, then!' jeered Cuthbert.

William, on all fours, disappeared into the mud and slime of the small round aperture. Joan clasped her hands, and even Cuthbert was secretly impressed. They stood in silence. At intervals William's muffled voice came from the tunnel.

'It's jolly muddy, too, I can *tell* you.'

'I've caught a frog! I say, I've caught a frog!'

'Crumbs! It's got away!'

'It's nearly quicksands here.'

'If I tried I could nearly *drown* here!'

At last, through the hedge, they saw him emerge in the field across the road. He swaggered across to them aglow with his own heroism. As he entered the gate he was rewarded by the old light of adoration in Joan's blue eyes, but on full sight of him it quickly turned to consternation. His appearance was beyond description. There was a malicious smile on Cuthbert's face.

'Do thumthing elth,' he urged him. 'Go on, do thumthing elth.'

'Oh, William,' said Joan anxiously, 'you'd better not.'

But the gods had sent madness to William. He was drunk with the sense of his own prowess. He was regardless of consequences.

He pointed to a little window high up in the coal-house.

'I can climb up that an' slide down the coal inside. That's what I can do. There's *nothin'* I can't do. I—'

'All right,' urged Cuthbert, 'if you can do that, do it, and I'll believe you can do anything.'

For Cuthbert, with unholy glee, foresaw William's undoing.

'Oh, William,' pleaded Joan, 'I *know* you're brave, but don't—'

'I CAN CLIMB UP THAT AN' SLIDE DOWN THE COAL INSIDE.
THAT'S WHAT I CAN DO. THERE'S NOTHIN' I CAN'T DO!'
SAID WILLIAM.

But William was already doing it. They saw his disappearance into the little window, they heard plainly his descent down the coal heap inside, and in less than a minute he appeared in the doorway. He was almost unrecognisable. Coal dust adhered freely to the moist consistency of the mud and lichen already clinging to his suit, as well as to his hair and face. His collar had been almost torn away from its stud. William himself was smiling proudly, utterly unconscious of his appearance. Joan was plainly wavering between horror and admiration. Then the moment for which Cuthbert had longed arrived.

'Children! Come in now!'

Cuthbert, clean and dainty, entered the drawing-room first and pointed an accusing finger at the strange figure which followed.

'He'th been climbing treeth an' crawling in the mud, an' rolling down the coalth. He'th a nathty rough boy.'

A wild babel arose as William entered.

'*William!*'

'You *dreadful* boy!'

'Joan, come right away from him. Come over here.'

'What *will* your father say?'

'William, my *carpet*!'

For the greater part of the stream's bed still clung to William's boots.

Doggedly William defended himself.

'I was showin' 'em how to do things. I was bein' a host. I was tryin' to make 'em *happy*! I—'

'William, don't stand there talking. Go straight upstairs to the bathroom.'

It was the end of the first battle, and undoubtedly William had lost. Yet William had caught sight of the smile on Cuthbert's face and William had decided that the smile was something to be avenged.

But fate did not favour him. Indeed, fate seemed to do the reverse.

The idea of a children's play did not emanate from William's mother, or Joan's. They were both free from guilt in that respect. It emanated from Mrs de Vere Carter. Mrs de Vere Carter was a neighbour with a genius for organisation. There were few things she did not organise till their every other aspect or aim was lost but that of 'organisation'. She also had what amounted practically to a disease for 'getting up' things. She 'got up' plays, and bazaars, and pageants, and concerts. There were, in fact, few things she did not 'get up'. It was the sight of Joan and Cuthbert walking together down the road, the sun shining on their golden curls, that had inspired her with the idea of 'getting up' a children's play. And Joan must be the Princess and little Cuthbert the Prince.

Mrs de Vere Carter was to write the play herself. At first she decided on Cinderella. Unfortunately there was a dearth of little girls in the neighbourhood, and therefore it was decided at a meeting composed of Mrs de Vere Carter, Mrs Clive, Mrs Brown (William's mother), and Ethel (William's sister), that William could easily be dressed up to represent one of the ugly sisters. It was, however, decided at a later meeting, consisting of William and his mother and sister, that William could not take the part. It was William who came to this decision. He was adamant against both threats and entreaties. Without cherishing any delusions about his personal appearance, he firmly declined to play the part of the ugly sister. They took the news with deep apologies to Mrs de Vere Carter, who was already in the middle of the first act. Her already low opinion of William sank to zero. Their next choice was Little Red Riding Hood, and William was lured, by glowing pictures of a realistic costume, into consenting to take the part of the Wolf. Every day he had to be dragged by some elder and responsible member of his family to a rehearsal. His hatred of Cuthbert was only equalled by his hatred of Mrs de Vere Carter.

'He acts so *unnaturally*,' moaned Mrs de Vere Carter. 'Try really to *think* you're a wolf, darling. Put some spirit into it. Be – *animated*.'

William scowled at her and once more muttered monotonously his opening lines:

A wolf am I – a wolf on mischief bent,
To eat this little maid is my intent.

'Take a breath after "bent", darling. Now say it again.'

William complied, introducing this time a loud and audible gasp to represent the breath. Mrs de Vere Carter sighed.

'Now, Cuthbert, darling, draw your little sword and put your arm round Joan. That's right.'

Cuthbert obeyed, and his clear voice rose in a high chanting monotone:

Avaunt! Begone! You wicked wolf, away!
This gentle maid shall never be your prey.

'That's beautiful, darling. Now, William, slink away. *Slink* away, darling. Don't stand staring at Cuthbert like that. Slink away. I'll show you. Watch me slink away.'

Mrs de Vere Carter slunk away realistically, and the sight of it brought momentary delight to William's weary soul. Otherwise the rehearsals were not far removed from torture to him. The thought of being a wolf had at first attracted him, but actually a wolf character who had to repeat Mrs de Vere Carter's meaningless couplets and be worsted at every turn by the smiling Cuthbert, who was forced to watch from behind the scenes the fond embraces of Cuthbert and Joan, galled his proud spirit unspeakably. Moreover, Cuthbert monopolised her both before and after the rehearsals.

'Come away, Joan, he'th prob'bly all over coal dutht and all of a meth.'

The continued presence of unsympathetic elders prevented his proper avenging of such insults.

The day of the performance approached, and there arose some little trouble about William's costume. If the wearing of the dining-room hearthrug had been forbidden by Authority it would have at once become the dearest wish of William's heart and a thing to be accomplished at all costs. But, because Authority decreed that that should be William's official costume as the Wolf, William at once began to find insuperable difficulties.

'It's a dirty ole thing, all dust and bits of black hair come off it on me. I don't think it *looks* like a wolf. Well, if I've gotter be a wolf folks might just as well *know* what I am. This looks like as if it came off a black sheep or sumthin'. You don't want folks to think I'm a *sheep* 'stead of a *wolf*, do you? You don't want me to be made look ridiclus before all these folks, do you?'

He was slightly mollified by their promise to hire a wolf's head for him. He practised wolf's howlings (though these had no part in Mrs de Vere Carter's play) at night in his room till he drove his family almost beyond the bounds of sanity.

Mrs de Vere Carter had hired the Village Hall for the performance, and the proceeds were to go to a local charity.

On the night of the play the Hall was packed, and Mrs de Vere Carter was in a flutter of excitement and im-portance.

'Yes, the dear children are splendid, and they look *beautiful*! We've all worked so *hard*. Yes, entirely my own composition. I only hope that William Brown won't *murder* my poetry as he does at rehearsals.'

The curtain went up.

The scene was a wood, as was evident from a few small branches of trees placed here and there at intervals on the stage.

Joan, in a white dress and red cloak, entered and began to speak, quickly and breathlessly, stressing every word with impartial regularity.

A little maid am I – Red Riding Hood,
My journey lies along this dark, thick wood.
Within my basket is a little jar
Of jam – a present for my grandmamma.

Then Cuthbert entered – a prince in white satin with a
blue sash. There was a rapt murmur of admiration in the
audience as he made his appearance.

William waited impatiently and uneasily behind the
scenes. His wolf's head was very hot. One of the eyeholes
was beyond his range of vision, through the other he had
a somewhat prescribed view of what went on around him.
He had been pinned tightly into the dining-room hearth-
rug, his arms pinioned down by his side. He was distinctly
uncomfortable.

At last his cue came.

Red Riding Hood and the Prince parted after a short
conversation in which their acquaintance made rapid
strides, and at the end of which the Prince said casually as
he turned to go:

So sweet a maid have I never seen,
Ere long I hope to make her my wife and queen.

Red Riding Hood gazed after him, remarking (all in the
same breath and tone):

The Rivals

How kind he is, how gentle and how good!
But, see what evil beast comes through the wood!

Here William entered amid wild applause. On the stage he
found that his one eyehole gave him an excellent view of
the audience. His mother and father were in the second
row. Turning his head round slowly he discovered his sister
Ethel sitting with a friend near the back.

'William,' hissed the prompter, 'go on! "A wolf am
I—"'

But William was engrossed in the audience. There was
Mrs Clive about the middle of the room.

'"A wolf am I" – *go on*, William!'

William had now found the cook and housemaid in the
last row of all and was turning his eyehole round in search
of fresh discoveries.

The prompter grew desperate.

'"A wolf am I – a wolf on mischief bent." *Say* it,
William.'

William turned his wolf's head towards the wings.
'Well, I was *goin'* to say it,' he said irritably, 'if you'd lef'
me alone.'

The audience tittered.

'Well, say it,' said the voice of the invisible prompter.

'Well, I'm going to,' said William. 'I'm not goin' to say

103

that again wot you said 'cause they all heard it. I'll go on from there.'

The audience rocked in wild delight. Behind the scenes Mrs de Vere Carter wrung her hands and sniffed strong smelling salts. 'That boy!' she moaned.

Then William, sinking his voice from the indignant clearness with which it had addressed the prompter, to a muffled inaudibility, continued:

To eat this little maid is my intent.

But there leapt on the stage again the radiant white and blue figure of the Prince brandishing his wooden sword.

Avaunt! Begone! You wicked wolf, away!
This gentle maid shall never be your prey.

At this point William should have slunk away. But the vision revealed by his one available eyehole of the Prince standing in a threatening attitude with one arm round Joan filled him with a sudden and unaccountable annoyance. He advanced slowly and pugnaciously towards the Prince; and the Prince, who had never before acted with William in his head (which was hired for one evening only) fled from the stage with a wild yell of fear. The curtain was lowered hastily.

There was consternation behind the scenes. William, glaring from out of his eyehole and refusing to remove his head, defended himself in his best manner.

'Well, I di'n't tell him to run away, did I? I di'n't *mean* him to run away. I only *looked* at him. Well, I was goin' to slink in a minit. I only wanted to look at him. I was *goin'* to slink.'

'Oh, never mind! Get on with the play!' moaned Mrs de Vere Carter. 'But you've quite destroyed the *atmosphere*, William. You've spoilt the beautiful story. But hurry up, it's time for the grandmother's cottage scene now.'

Not a word of William's speeches was audible in the next scene, but his attack on and consumption of the aged grandmother was one of the most realistic parts of the play, especially considering the fact that his arms were imprisoned.

'Not so roughly, William!' said the prompter in a sibilant whisper. 'Don't make so much noise. They can't hear a word anyone's saying.'

At last William was clothed in the nightgown and nightcap and lying in the bed ready for little Red Riding Hood's entrance. The combined effect of the rug and the head and the thought of Cuthbert had made him hotter and crosser than he ever remembered having felt before. He was conscious of a wild and unreasoning indignation against the world in general. Then Joan entered and began to pipe monotonously:

Dear grandmamma, I've come with all quickness
To comfort you and soothe your bed of sickness.
Here are some little dainties I have brought
To show you how we cherish you in our thought.

Here William wearily rose from his bed and made an unconvincing spring in her direction.

But on the stage leapt Cuthbert once more, the vision in blue and white with golden curls shining and sword again drawn.

'Ha! Evil beast—'

It was too much for William. The heat and discomfort of his attire, the sight of the hated Cuthbert already about to embrace *his* Joan, goaded him to temporary madness. With a furious gesture he burst the pins which attached the dining-room hearthrug to his person and freed his arms. He tore off the white nightgown. He sprang at the petrified Cuthbert – a small wild figure in a jersey suit and a wolf's head.

Mrs de Vere Carter had filled Red Riding Hood's basket with packages of simple groceries, which included, among other things, a paper bag of flour and a jar of jam.

William seized these wildly and hurled handfuls of

flour at the prostrate, screaming Cuthbert. The stage was suddenly pandemonium. The other small actors promptly joined the battle. The prompter was too panic stricken to lower the curtain. The air was white with clouds of flour. The victim scrambled to his feet and fled, a ghost-like figure, round the table.

'Take him off me,' he yelled. 'Take him *off* me. Take William off me.' His wailing was deafening.

The next second he was on the floor, with William on top of him. William now varied the proceedings by emptying the jar of jam on to Cuthbert's face and hair.

They were separated at last by the prompter and stage manager, while the audience rose and cheered hysterically. But louder than the cheering rose the sound of Cuthbert's lamentation.

'He'th a nathty, rough boy! He puthed me down. He'th methed my nith clotheth. Boo-hoo!'

Mrs de Vere Carter was inarticulate.

'That boy . . . that *boy* . . . *that boy*!' was all she could say.

William was hurried away by his family before she could regain speech.

'You're disgraced us publicly,' said Mrs Brown plaintively. 'I thought you must have gone *mad*. People will never forget it. I might have known . . .'

THE SIGHT OF THE HATED CUTHBERT ABOUT TO EMBRACE
HIS JOAN GOADED WILLIAM TO TEMPORARY MADNESS.

When pressed for an explanation, William would only say:

'Well, I felt hot. I felt awful hot, an' I di'n't like Cuthbert.'

He appeared to think this sufficient explanation, though he was fully prepared for the want of sympathy displayed by his family.

'Well,' he said firmly, 'I'd just like to see you do it, I'd just like to see you be in the head and that ole rug an' have to say stupid things an' – an' see folks you don't like, an' I bet you'd *do* something.'

But he felt that public feeling was against him, and relapsed sadly into silence. From the darkness in front of them came the sound of Cuthbert's wailing as Mrs Clive led her two charges home.

'*Poor* little Cuthbert!' said Mrs Brown. 'If I were Joan, I don't think I'd ever speak to you again.'

'Huh!' ejaculated William scornfully.

But at William's gate a small figure slipped out from the darkness and two little arms crept round William's neck.

'Oh, *William*,' she whispered, 'he's going tomorrow, and I'm glad. Isn't he a softie? Oh, William, I do *love* you, you do such '*citing* things!'

CHAPTER 7

THE GHOST

William lay on the floor of the barn, engrossed in a book. This was a rare thing with William. His bottle of lemonade lay untouched by his side, and he even forgot the half-eaten apple which reposed in his hand. His jaws were arrested midway in the act of munching.

'Our hero,' he read, 'was awakened about midnight by the sound of the rattling of chains. Raising himself on his arm he gazed into the darkness. About a foot from his bed he could discern a tall, white, faintly gleaming figure and a ghostly arm which beckoned him.'

William's hair stood on end.

'Crumbs!' he ejaculated.

'Nothing perturbed,' he continued to read, 'our hero rose and followed the spectre through the long winding passages of the old castle. Whenever he hesitated, a white, luminous arm, hung around with ghostly chains, beckoned him on.'

'Gosh!' murmured the enthralled William. 'I'd have bin scared!'

'At the panel in the wall the ghost stopped, and silently the panel slid aside, revealing a flight of stone steps. Down this went the apparition followed by our intrepid hero. There was a small stone chamber at the bottom, and into this the rays of moonlight poured, revealing a skeleton in a sitting attitude beside a chest of golden sovereigns. The gold gleamed in the moonlight.'

'Golly!' gasped William, red with excitement.

'William!'

The cry came from somewhere in the sunny garden outside. William frowned sternly, took another bite of apple, and continued to read.

'Our hero gave a cry of astonishment.'

'Yes, I'd have done that all right,' agreed William.

'*William!*'

'Oh, shut *up*!' called William, irritably, thereby revealing his hiding place.

His grown-up sister, Ethel, appeared in the doorway.

'Mother wants you,' she announced.

'Well, I can't come. I'm busy,' said William, coldly, taking a draught of lemonade and returning to his book.

'Cousin Mildred's come,' continued his sister.

William raised his freckled face from his book.

'Well, I can't help that, can I?' he said, with the air of one arguing patiently with a lunatic.

Ethel shrugged her shoulders and departed.

'He's reading some old book in the barn,' he heard her announce, 'and he says—'

Here he foresaw the complications and hastily followed her.

'Well, I'm *comin'*, aren't I?' he said. 'As fast as I can.'

Cousin Mildred was sitting on the lawn. She was elderly and very thin and very tall, and she wore a curious, long, shapeless garment of green silk with a golden girdle.

'Dear child!' she murmured, taking the grimy hand that William held out to her in dignified silence.

He was cheered by the sight of tea and hot cakes.

Cousin Mildred ate little but talked much.

'I'm living in *hopes* of a psychic revelation, dear,' she said to William's mother. '*In hopes!* I've heard of wonderful experiences, but so far none – alas! – have befallen me. Automatic writing I have tried, but any communication the spirits may have sent me that way remained illegible – quite illegible.'

She sighed.

William eyed her with scorn while he consumed reckless quantities of hot cakes.

'I would *love* to have a psychic revelation,' she sighed again.

'Yes, dear,' murmured Mrs Brown, mystified. 'William, you've had enough.'

'*Enough?*' said William in surprise. 'Why I've only had—' He decided hastily against exact statistics and in favour of vague generalities.

ETHEL APPEARED IN THE DOORWAY. 'MOTHER WANTS YOU,' SHE ANNOUNCED.

'I've only had hardly any,' he said aggrievedly.

'You've had *enough*, anyway,' said Mrs Brown firmly. The martyr rose, pale but proud.

'Well, can I go then, if I can't have any more tea?'

'There's plenty of bread and butter.'

'I don't want bread and butter,' he said, scornfully.

'Dear child!' murmured Cousin Mildred, vaguely, as he departed.

He returned to the story and lemonade and apple, and stretched himself happily at full length in the shady barn.

'But the ghostly visitant seemed to be fading away, and with a soft sigh was gone. Our hero, with a start of surprise, realised that he was alone with the gold and the skeleton. For the first time he experienced a thrill of cold fear and slowly retreated up the stairs before the hollow and, as it seemed, vindictive stare of the grinning skeleton.'

'I wonder wot he was grinnin' at?' said William.

'But to his horror the door was shut, the panel had slid back. He had no means of opening it. He was imprisoned on a remote part of the castle, where even the servants came but rarely, and at intervals of weeks. Would his fate be that of the man whose bones gleamed white in the moonlight?'

'Crumbs!' said William, earnestly.

Then a shadow fell upon the floor of the barn, and Cousin Mildred's voice greeted him.

'So you're here, dear? I'm just exploring your garden and thinking. I like to be alone. I see that you are the same, dear child!'

'I'm readin',' said William, with icy dignity.

'Dear boy! Won't you come and show me the garden and your favourite nooks and corners?'

William looked at her thin, vague, amiable face, and shut his book with a resigned sigh.

'All right,' he said, laconically.

He conducted her in patient silence round the kitchen garden and the shrubbery. She looked sadly at the house, with its red brick, uncompromisingly modern appearance.

'William, I wish your house was *old*,' she said sadly.

William resented any aspersions on his house from outsiders. Personally he considered newness in a house an attraction, but, if anyone wished for age, then old his house should be.

'*Old!*' he ejaculated. 'Huh! I guess it's *old* enough.'

'Oh, is it?' she said, delighted. 'Restored recently, I suppose?'

'Umph,' agreed William, nodding.

'Oh, I'm so glad. I may have some psychic revelation here, then?'

'Oh yes,' said William, judicially. 'I shouldn't wonder.'

'William, have you ever had one?'

'Well,' said William, guardedly, 'I dunno.'

His mysterious manner threw her into a transport.

'Of course not to anyone. But to *me* – I'm one of the sympathetic! To me you may speak freely, William.'

William, feeling that his ignorance could no longer be hidden by words, maintained a discreet silence.

'To me it shall be sacred, William. I will tell no one – not even your parents. I believe that children see – clouds of glory and all that,' she said vaguely. 'With your unstained childish vision—'

'I'm eleven,' put in William indignantly.

'You see things that to the wise are sealed. Some manifestation, some spirit, some ghostly visitant—'

'Oh,' said William, suddenly enlightened, 'you talkin' about *ghosts*?'

'Yes, ghosts, William.'

Her air of deference flattered him. She evidently expected great things of him. Great things she should have. At the best of times with William imagination was stronger than cold facts.

He gave a short laugh.

'Oh, *ghosts*! Yes, I've seen some of 'em. I guess I *have*!'
Her face lit up.

'Will you tell me some of your experiences, William?'
she said, humbly.

'Well,' said William, loftily, 'you won't go *talkin'* about
it, will you?'

'Oh, *no*.'

'Well, I've seem 'em, you know. Chains an' all. And
skeletons. And ghostly arms beckonin' an' all that.'

William was enjoying himself. He walked with a swagger. He almost believed what he said. She gasped.

'Oh, go on!' she said. 'Tell me all.'

He went on. He soared aloft on the wings of imagination, his hands in his pockets, his freckled face puckered
up in frowning mental effort. He certainly enjoyed himself.

'If only some of it could happen to *me*,' breathed his
confidante. 'Does it come to you at *nights*, William?'

'Yes,' nodded William. 'Nights mostly.'

'I shall – watch tonight,' said Cousin Mildred. 'And
you say the house is old?'

'Awful old,' said William, reassuringly.

Her attitude to William was a relief to the rest of the
family. Visitors sometimes objected to William.

'She seems to have almost taken to William,' said his

mother, with a note of unflattering incredulity in her voice.

William was pleased yet embarrassed by her attentions. It was a strange experience to him to be accepted by a grown-up as a fellow being. She talked to him with interest and a certain humility, she bought him sweets and seemed pleased that he accepted them, she went for walks with him, and evidently took his constrained silence for the silence of depth and wisdom.

Beneath his embarrassment he was certainly pleased and flattered. She seemed to prefer his company to that of Ethel. That was one in the eye for Ethel. But he felt that something was expected from him in return for all this kindness and attention. William was a sportsman. He decided to supply it. He took a book of ghost stories from the juvenile library at school, and read them in the privacy of his room at night. Many were the thrilling adventures which he had to tell Cousin Mildred in the morning. Cousin Mildred's bump of credulity was a large one. She supplied him with sweets on a generous scale. She listened to him with awe and wonder.

'William . . . you are one of the elect, the chosen,' she said, 'one of those whose spirits can break down the barrier between the unseen world and ours with ease.' And always she sighed and stroked back her thin locks, sadly.

'Oh, how I wish that some experience would happen to *me*!'

One morning, after the gift of an exceptionally large tin of toffee, William's noblest feelings were aroused. Manfully he decided that something *should* happen to her.

Cousin Mildred slept in the bedroom above William's. Descent from one window to the other was easy, but ascent was difficult. That night Cousin Mildred awoke suddenly as the clock struck twelve. There was no moon, and only dimly did she discern the white figure that stood in the light of the window. She sat up, quivering with eagerness. Her short, thin little pigtail stuck out horizontally from her head. Her mouth was wide open.

'Oh!' she gasped.

The white figure moved a step forward and coughed nervously.

Cousin Mildred clasped her hands.

'Speak!' she said, in a tense whisper. 'Oh, speak! Some message! Some revelation!'

William was nonplussed. None of the ghosts he had read of had spoken. They had rattled and groaned and beckoned, but they had not spoken. He tried groaning and emitted a sound faintly reminiscent of a seasick voyager.

'Oh, *speak*!' pleaded Cousin Mildred.

Evidently speech was a necessary part of this performance. William wondered whether ghosts spoke English or a language of their own. He inclined to the latter view and nobly took the plunge.

'Honk. Yonk. Ponk,' he said, firmly.

Cousin Mildred gasped in wonder.

'Oh, explain,' she pleaded, ardently. 'Explain in our poor human speech. Some message—'

William took fright. It was all turning out to be much more complicated than he had expected. He hastily passed through the room and out of the door, closing it noisily behind him. As he ran along the passage came sound came like a crash of thunder. Outside in the passage were Cousin Mildred's boots, William's father's boots, and William's brother's boots, and into these charged William in his headlong retreat. They slid noisily along the polished wooden surface of the floor, ricocheting into each other as they went. Doors opened suddenly and William's father collided with William's brother in the dark passage, where they wrestled fiercely before they discovered each other's identity.

'I heard that confounded noise and I came out—'

'So did I.'

'Well, then, who *made* it?'

The Ghost

SHE SAT UP, QUIVERING WITH EAGERNESS. HER SHORT,
THIN LITTLE PIGTAIL STUCK OUT HORIZONTALLY FROM
HER HEAD. HER MOUTH WAS WIDE OPEN.

'Who did?'

'If it's that wretched boy up to any tricks again—'

William's father left the sentence unfinished, but went with determined tread towards his younger son's room. William was discovered, carefully spreading a sheet over his bed and smoothing it down.

Mr Brown, roused from his placid slumbers, was a sight to make a brave man quail, but the glance that William turned upon him was guileless and sweet.

'Did you make that confounded row kicking boots about the passage?' spluttered the man of wrath.

'No, Father,' said William, gently. 'I've not bin kickin' no boots about.'

'Were you down on the lower landing just now?' said Mr Brown, with compressed fury.

William considered this question silently for a few seconds, then spoke up brightly and innocently.

'I dunno, Father. You see, some folks walk in their sleep, and when they wake up they dunno where they've bin. Why, I've heard of a man walkin' down a fire escape in his sleep, and then he woke up and couldn't think how he'd got to be there where he was. You see, he didn't know he'd walked down all them steps sound asleep, and—'

'Be *quiet*,' thundered his father. 'What in the name

of— What on earth are you doing making your bed in the middle of the night? Are you insane?'

William, perfectly composed, tucked in one end of his sheet.

'No, Father, I'm not insane. My sheet just fell off me in the night and I got out to pick it up. I must of bin a bit restless, I suppose. Sheets come off easy when folks is restless in bed, and they don't know anythin' about it till they wake up jus' same as sleepwalkin'. Why, I've heard of folks—'

'Be *quiet*—'

At that moment William's mother arrived, placid as ever, in her dressing gown, carrying a candle.

'Look at him,' said Mr Brown, pointing at the meek-looking William.

'He plays rugger up and down the passage with the boots all night and then he begins to make his bed. He's mad. He's—'

William turned his calm gaze upon him.

'*I* wasn't playin' rugger with the boots, Father,' he said, patiently.

Mrs Brown laid her hand soothingly upon her husband's arm.

'You know, dear,' she said, gently, 'a house is always full of noises at night. Basket chairs creaking—'

Mr Brown's face grew purple.

'*Basket chairs*—' he exploded, violently, but allowed himself to be led unresisting from the room.

William finished his bed-making with his usual frown of concentration, then, lying down, fell at once into the deep sleep of childish innocence.

But Cousin Mildred was lying awake, a blissful smile upon her lips. She, too, was now one of the elect, the chosen. Her rather deaf ears had caught the sound of supernatural thunder as her ghostly visitant departed, and she had beamed with ecstatic joy.

'Honk,' she murmured dreamily. 'Honk. Yonk. Ponk.'

William felt rather tired the next evening. Cousin Mildred had departed leaving him a handsome present of a large box of chocolates. William had consumed these with undue haste in view of possible maternal interference. His broken night was telling upon his spirits. He felt distinctly depressed and saw the world through jaundiced eyes. He sat in the shrubbery, his chin in his hand, staring moodily at his adoring mongrel, Jumble.

'It's a rotten world,' he said, gloomily. 'I've took a lot of trouble over her and she goes and makes me feel sick with chocolates.'

Jumbled wagged his tail, sympathetically.

CHAPTER 8

THE MAY KING

William was frankly bored. School always bored him. He disliked facts, and he disliked being tied down to detail, and he disliked answering questions. As a politician a great future would have lain before him. William attended a mixed school because his parents hoped that feminine influence might have a mellowing effect upon his character. As yet the mellowing was not apparent. He was roused from his daydreams by a change in the voice of Miss Dewhurst, his form mistress. It was evident that she was not talking about the exports of England (a subject in which William took little interest) any longer.

'Children,' she said brightly. 'I want you to have a little May Queen for the first of May. The rest of you must be her courtiers. I want you all to vote tomorrow. Put down on a piece of paper the name of the little girl you think would make the sweetest little Queen, and the rest of you shall be her swains and maidens.'

'We're goin' to have a May Queen,' remarked William to his family at dinner, 'an' I'm goin' to be a swain.'

His interested died down considerably when he discovered the meaning of the word swain.

'Isn't it no sort of animal at all?' he asked indignantly.

'Well, I'm not going to be in it, then,' he said when he heard that it was not.

The next morning Evangeline Fish began to canvass for votes methodically. Evangeline Fish was very fair, and was dressed always in that shade of blue that shrieks aloud to the heavens and puts the skies to shame. She was considered the beauty of the form.

'I'll give you two bull's eyes if you'll vote for me,' she said to William.

'*Two!*' said William with scorn.

'Six,' she bargained.

'All right,' he said, 'you can give me six bull's eyes if you want. There's nothing to stop you givin' me six bull's eyes if you want, is there? Not that I know of.'

'But you'll have to promise to put down my name on the paper if I give you six bull's eyes,' she said suspiciously.

'All right,' said William. 'I can easy promise that.'

Whereupon she handed over the six bull's eyes. William returned one as being under regulation size, and waited frowning till she replaced it by a larger one.

'Now, you've promised,' said Evangeline Fish. 'They'll make you ill an' die if you break your promise on them.'

William kept his promise with true political address. He wrote 'E. Fish – I *don't* think!' on his voting paper and his vote was disqualified. But Evangeline Fish was elected May Queen by an overwhelming majority. She was, after all, the beauty of the form and she always wore blue. And now she was to be May Queen. Her prestige was established for ever. 'Little angel,' murmured the elder girls. The small boys fought for her favours. William began to dislike her intensely. Her voice, and her smile, and her ringlets, and her blue dress began to jar upon his nerves. And when anything began to jar on William's nerves something always happened.

It was not till about a week later that he noticed Bettine Franklin. Bettine was small and dark. There was nothing 'angelic' about her. William had noticed her vaguely in school before and had hardly looked upon her as a distinct personality. But one recreation in the playground he stood leaning against the wall by himself, scowling at Evangeline Fish. She was surrounded by a crowd of admirers, and was prattling to them artlessly in her angelic voice.

'I'm going to be dressed in white muslin with a blue sash. Blue suits me, you know. I'm so fair.' She tossed back a ringlet. 'One of you will have to hold my train and the rest must dance round me. I'm going to have a crown and—' She turned round in order to avoid the scowling gaze of William in the distance. William had discovered that his scowl annoyed her, and since then had given it little rest. But there was no satisfaction in scowling at the back of her well-curled head, so he relaxed his scowl and let his gaze wander round the playground. And it fell upon Bettine. Bettine was also standing by herself and gazing at Evangeline Fish. But she was not scowling. She was looking at Evangeline Fish with wistful envy. For Evangeline Fish was 'angelic' and a May Queen, and she was neither of these things. William strolled over and lolled against the wall next to her.

''Ullo!' he said, without looking at her, for this change of position had brought him again within range of Evangeline Fish's eye, and he was once more simply one concentrated scowl.

''Ullo,' murmured Bettine shyly and politely.

'You like pink rock?' was William's next effort.

'Um,' said Bettine, nodding emphatically.

'I'll give you some next time I buy some,' said William munificently, 'but I shan't be buying any for a long time,' he added bitterly, ''cause an ole ball slipped out my hands on to our dining-room window before I noticed it yesterday.'

She nodded understandingly.

'I don't mind!' she said sweetly. 'I'll like you jus' as much if you don't give me any rock.'

William blushed.

'I di'n't know you liked me,' he said.

'I do,' she said fervently. 'I like your face an' I like the things you say.'

William had forgotten to scowl. He was one flaming mixture of embarrassment and delight. He plunged his hands into his pockets and brought out two marbles, a piece of clay, and a broken toy gun.

'You can have 'em all,' he said in reckless generosity.

'You keep 'em for me,' said Bettine sweetly. 'I hope you dance next to me at the maypole when Evangeline's Queen. Won't it be lovely?' and she sighed.

'Lovely?' exploded William. 'Huh!'

'Won't you like it?' said Bettine wonderingly.

'*Me!*' exploded William again. 'Dancin' round a pole! Round that ole girl?'

'But she's so pretty.'

'No, she isn't,' said William firmly, 'she jus' isn't. Not *much*! I don' like her narsy shiny hair an' I don't like her narsy blue clothes, an' I don' like her narsy face, an' I don't like her narsy white shoes, nor her narsy necklaces, nor her narsy squeaky voice—'

He paused.

Bettine drew a deep breath.

'Go on some more,' she said. 'I *like* listening to you.'

'Do *you* like her?' said William.

'No. She's awful *greedy*. Did you know she was awful *greedy*?'

'I can *b'lieve* it,' said William. 'I can b'lieve *anything* of anyone wot talks in that squeaky voice.'

'Jus' watch her when she's eatin' cakes – she goes on eatin' and eatin' and eatin'.'

'She'll bust an' die one day then,' prophesied William solemnly, 'an' *I* shan't be sorry.'

'But she'll look ever so beautiful when she's a May Queen.'

'You'd look nicer,' said William.

Bettine's small pale face flamed.

'Oh, *no*,' she said.

'Would you like to be a May Queen?'

'Oh, *yes*,' she said.

'Um,' said William, and returned to the discomfiture of Evangeline Fish by his steady concentrated scowl.

The next day he had the opportunity of watching her eating cakes. They met at the birthday party of a mutual classmate, and Evangeline Fish took her stand by the table and consumed cakes with a perseverance and determination worthy of a nobler cause. William accorded her a

certain grudging admiration. Not once did she falter or
faint. Iced cakes, cream cakes, pastries melted away
before her and never did she lose her ethereal angelic
appearance. Tight golden ringlets, blue eyes, faintly
flushed cheeks, vivid pale blue dress remained immaculate
and unruffled, and still she ate cakes. William watched
her in amazement, forgetting even to scowl at her. Her

WILLIAM ACCORDED HER A CERTAIN GRUDGING
ADMIRATION. ICED CAKES, CREAM CAKES, PASTRIES
MELTED AWAY BEFORE HER.

capacity for cakes exceeded even William's, and his was no mean one.

They had a rehearsal of the maypole dance and crowning the next day.

'I want William Brown to hold the Queen's train,' said Miss Dewhurst.

'*Me?*' ejaculated William in horror. 'D'you mean *me?*'

'Yes, dear. It's a great honour to be asked to hold little Queen Evangeline's train. I'm sure you feel very proud. You must be her little courtier.'

'Huh!' said William, transferring his scowl to Miss Dewhurst.

Evangeline beamed. She wanted William's admiration. William was the only boy in the form who was not her slave. She smiled at William sweetly.

'I'm not *good* at holdin' trains,' said William. 'I don't *like* holdin' trains. I've never bin *taught* 'bout holdin' trains. I might do it wrong on the day an' spoil it all. I shan't like to spoil it all,' he added virtuously.

'Oh, we'll have heaps of practices,' said Miss Dewhurst brightly.

As he was going Bettine pressed a small apple into his hand.

'A present for you,' she murmured. 'I saved it from my dinner.'

The May King

He was touched.

'I'll give you somethin' tomorrow,' he said, adding hastily, 'if I can find anythin'.'

They stood in silence till he had finished his apple.

'I've left a lot on the core,' he said in a tone of unusual politeness, handing it to her, 'would you like to finish it?'

'No, thank you. William, you'll look so nice holding her train.'

'I don't want to, an' I bet I *won't*! You don't *know* the things I can do,' he said darkly.

'Oh, William!' she gasped in awe and admiration.

'I'd hold your train if you was goin' to be queen,' he volunteered.

'I wouldn't want you to hold my train,' she said earnestly. 'I'd – I'd – I'd want you to be May King with me.'

'Yes. Why don't they have May Kings?' said William, stung by this insult to his sex.

'Why shouldn't there be a May King?'

'I speck they *do*, really, only p'raps Miss Dewhurst doesn't know about it.'

'Well, it doesn't seem sense not having May Kings, does it? I wun't mind bein' May King if you was May Queen.'

*

The rehearsal was, on the whole, a failure.

'William Brown, don't hold the train so high. No, not quite so low. Don't stand so near the Queen, William Brown. No, not so far away – you'll pull the train off. Walk when the Queen walks, William Brown, don't stand still. Sing up, please, train-bearer. No, not quite so loud. That's deafening and not melodious.'

In the end he was degraded from the position of train-bearer to that of ordinary 'swain'. The 'swains' were to be dressed in smocks and the 'maidens' in print dresses, and the maypole dance was to be performed round Evangeline Fish, who was to stand in queenly attire by the pole in the middle. All the village was to be invited.

At the end of the rehearsal William came upon Bettine, once more gazing wistfully at Evangeline Fish, who was coquetting (with many tosses of the fair ringlets) before a crowd of admirers.

'Isn't it lovely for her to be May Queen?' said Bettine.

'She's a rotten one,' said William. 'I'm jolly glad *I've* not to hold up her rotten ole train an' listen to her narsy squeaky voice singin' close to, an' I'll give you a present to-morrow.'

He did. He found a centipede in the garden and pressed it into her hand on the way to school.

'They're jolly int'restin',' he said. 'Put it in a matchbox and make holes for its breath and it'll live ever so long. It won't bite you if you hold it the right way.'

And because she loved William she took it without even a shudder.

Evangeline Fish began to pursue William. She grudged him bitterly to Bettine. She pirouetted near him in her sky-blue garments, she tossed her ringlets about him. She ogled him with her pale blue eyes.

And in the long school hours during which he dreamed at his desk, or played games with his friends, while highly paid instructors poured forth their wisdom for his benefit, William evolved a plan. Unfortunately, like most plans, it required capital, and William had no capital. Occasionally William's elder brother Robert would supply a few shillings without inconvenient questions, but it happened that Robert was ignoring William's existence at that time. For Robert had (not for the first time) discovered his Ideal, and the Ideal had been asked to lunch the previous week. For days before Robert had made William's life miserable. He had objected to William's unbrushed hair and unmanicured hands, and untidy person, and noisy habits. He had bitterly demanded what She would think on being asked to a house where She might meet such an individual as William; he had insisted that William should be taught habits of cleanliness and silence before She came; he had

hinted darkly that a man who had William for a brother
was hampered considerably in his love affairs because She
would think it was a queer kind of family where anyone
like William was allowed to grow up. He had reserved
some of his fervour for the cook. She must have a proper
lunch – not stews and stuff they often had – there must be
three vegetables and there must be cheese straws. Cook
must learn to make better cheese straws. And William,
having swallowed insults for three whole days, planned
vengeance. It was a vengeance which only William could
have planned or carried out. For only William could have
seized a moment just before lunch when the meal was
dished up and Cook happened to be out of the kitchen to
carry the principal dishes down to the coal cellar and conceal them beneath the best nuts.

It is well to draw a veil over the next half-hour. Both
William and the meal had vanished. Robert tore his hair
and appealed vainly to the heavens. He hinted darkly at
suicide. For what is cold tongue and coffee to offer to an
Ideal? The meal was discovered during the afternoon in its
resting place and given to William's mongrel, Jumble, who
crept about during the next few days in agonies of indi-
gestion. Robert had bitterly demanded of William why he
went about the world spoiling people's lives and ruining
their happiness. He had implied that when William met

with the One and Only Love of his Life he need look for no help or assistance from him (Robert), because he (William) had dashed to the ground his (Robert's) cup of happiness, because he'd never in his life met anyone before like Miss Laing, and never would again, and he (William) had simply condemned him to a lonely and miserable old age, because who'd want to marry anyone that asked them to lunch and then gave them coffee and cold tongue, and he'd never want to marry anyone else, because it was the One and Only Love of his Life, and he hoped he (William) would realise, when he was old enough to realise, what it meant to have your life spoilt and your happiness ruined all through coffee and tongue, because someone you'd never speak to again had hidden the lunch. Whence it came that William, optimist though he was, felt that any appeal to Robert for funds would be inopportune, to say the least of it.

But Providence was on William's side for once. An old uncle came to tea and gave William five shillings.

'Going to dance at a maypole, I hear?' he chuckled.

'P'raps,' was all William said.

His family were relieved by his meekness with regard to the May Day festival. Sometimes William made such a foolish fuss about being dressed up and performing in public.

'You know, dear,' said his mother, 'it's a dear old festival, and quite an honour to take part in it, and a smock is quite a nice manly garment.'

'Yes, Mother,' said William.

The day was fine – a real May Day. The maypole was fixed up in the field near the school, and the little performers were to change in the schoolroom.

William went out with his brown paper parcel of stage properties under his arm and stood gazing up the road by which Evangeline Fish must come to the school. For Evangeline Fish would have to pass his gate. Soon he saw her, her pale blue dress radiant in the sun.

''Ullo!' he greeted her.

She simpered. She had won him at last.

'Waitin' to walk to the school with me, William?' she said.

He still loitered.

'You're awful early.'

'Am I? I thought I was late. I meant to be late. I don't want to be too early. I'm the most 'portant person, and I want to walk in after the others, then they'll all look at me.'

She tossed her tightly wrought curls.

'Come into our ole shed a minute,' said William. 'I've got a present for you.'

She blushed and ogled.

'Oh, *William*!' she said, and followed him into the woodshed.

'Look!' he said.

His uncle's five shillings had been well expended. Rows of cakes lay round the shed; pastries, and sugar cakes, and iced cakes, and currant cakes.

'Have a lot,' said William. 'They're all for you. Go on! Eat 'em all. You can eat an' eat an' eat. There's lots an' lots of time and they can't begin without you, can they?'

'Oh, *William*!' she said.

She gloated over them.

'Oh, may I?'

'There's heaps of time,' said William. 'Go on! Eat them all!'

Her greedy little eyes seemed to stand out of her head.

'Oo!' she said in rapture.

She sat down on the floor and began to eat, lost to everything but icing and currants and pastry. William made for the door, then he paused, gazed wistfully at the feast, stepped back, and, grabbing a cream bun in each hand, crept quietly away.

Bettine in her print frock was at the door of the school.

'Hurry up!' she said anxiously. 'You're going to be late. The others are all out. They're waiting to begin. Miss

'HAVE A LOT,' SAID WILLIAM. 'THEY'RE ALL FOR YOU. GO
ON! EAT 'EM ALL. YOU CAN EAT AN' EAT AN' EAT.'

Dewhurst's out there. They're all come but you an' the
Queen. I stayed 'cause you asked me to stay to help you.'

He came in and shut the door.

'You're goin' to be May Queen,' he announced firmly.

'*Me?*' she said in amazement.

'Yes. An' I'm goin' to be King.'

He unwrapped his parcel.

'Look!' he said.

He had ransacked his sister's bedroom. Once Ethel had been to a fancy-dress dance as a fairy. Over Bettine's print frock he drew a crumpled gauze slip with wings, torn in several places. On her brow he placed a tinsel crown at a rakish angle. And she quivered with happiness.

'Oh, how lovely!' she said. 'How lovely! How lovely!'

His own preparations were simpler. He tied a red sash that he had taken off his sister's hat over his right shoulder and under his left arm on the top of his smock. Someone had once given him a small bus conductor's cap with a toy set of tickets and clippers. He placed the cap upon his head with its peak over one eye. It was the only official headgear he had been able to procure. Then he took a piece of burnt cork from his parcel and solemnly drew a fierce and military moustache upon his cheek and lip. To William no kind of theatricals was complete without a corked moustache.

Then he took Bettine by the hand and led her out to the maypole.

The dancers were all waiting holding the ribbons. The audience was assembled and a murmur of conversation was rising from it. It ceased abruptly as William and

Bettine appeared. William's father, mother and sister were in the front row. Robert was not there. Robert had declined to come to anything in which that little wretch was to perform. He'd jolly well had enough of that little wretch to last his lifetime, thank you very much.

William and Bettine stepped solemnly hand in hand upon the little platform which had been provided for the May Queen.

Miss Dewhurst, who was chatting amicably to the parents till the last of her small performers should appear, seemed suddenly turned to stone, with mouth gaping and eyes wide. The old fiddler, who was rather short-sighted, struck up the strains, and the dancers began to dance. The audience relaxed, leaning back in their chairs to enjoy the scene. Miss Dewhurst was still frozen. There were murmured comments. 'How curious to have that boy there! A sort of attendant, I suppose.'

'Yes, perhaps he's something allegorical. A sort of pageant. Good Luck or something. It's not quite the sort of thing I expected, I must admit.'

'What do you think of the Queen's dress? I always thought Miss Dewhurst had better taste. Rather tawdry, I call it.'

'I think the moustache is a mistake. It gives quite a common look to the whole thing. I wonder who he's meant to be? Pan, do you think?' uncertainly.

'Oh, no, nothing so *pagan*, I hope,' said an elderly matron, horrified. 'He's that Brown boy, you know. There always seems to be something queer about anything he's in. I've noticed it often. But I *hope* he's meant to be

WILLIAM AND BETTINE STEPPED SOLEMNLY HAND IN
HAND UPON THE LITTLE PLATFORM WHICH HAD BEEN
PROVIDED FOR THE MAY QUEEN.

something more Christian than Pan, though one never knows these days,' she added darkly.

William's sister had recognised her possessions, and was gasping in anger.

William's father, who knew William, was smiling sardonically.

William's mother was smiling proudly.

'You're always running William down,' she said to the world in general, 'but look at him now. He's got a very important part, and he said nothing about it at home. I call it very nice and modest of him. And what a dear little girl.'

Bettine, standing on the platform with William's hand holding hers and the maypole dancers dancing round her, was radiant with pride and happiness.

And Evangeline Fish in the woodshed was just beginning the last currant cake.

CHAPTER 9

THE REVENGE

William was a scout. The fact was well known. There was no one within a five-mile radius of William's home who did not know it. Sensitive old ladies had fled shuddering from their front windows when William marched down the street singing (the word is a euphemism) his scout songs in his strong young voice. Curious smells emanated from the depth of the garden where William performed mysterious culinary operations. One old lady whose cat had disappeared looked at William with dour suspicion in her eyes whenever he passed. Even the return of her cat a few weeks later did not remove the hostility from her gaze whenever it happened to rest upon William.

William's family had welcomed the suggestion of William's becoming a scout.

'It will keep him out of mischief,' they had said.

They were notoriously optimistic where William was concerned.

William's elder brother only was doubtful.

'You know what William is,' he said, and in that dark saying much was contained.

Things went fairly smoothly for some time. He took the scout's law of a daily deed of kindness in its most literal sense. He was to do one (and one only) deed of kindness a day. There were times when he forced complete strangers, much to their embarrassment, to be the unwilling recipients of his deed of kindness. There were times when he answered any demand for help with a cold: 'No, I've done it today.'

He received with saint-like patience the eloquence of his elder sister when she found her silk scarf tied into innumerable knots.

'Well, they're jolly good knots,' was all he said.

He had been looking forward to the holidays for a long time. He was to 'go under canvas' at the end of the first week.

The first day of the holidays began badly. William's father had been disturbed by William, whose room was just above and who had spent most of the night performing gymnastics as instructed by his scoutmaster.

'No, he didn't *say* do it at nights, but he said do it. He said it would make us grow up strong men. Don't you *want* me to grow up a strong man? He's ever so strong an' *he* did 'em. Why shun't I?'

146

His mother found a pan with the bottom burnt out and at once accused William of the crime. William could not deny it.

'Well, I was makin' sumthin', sumthin' he'd told us an' I forgot it. Well, I've *got* to make things if I'm a scout. I didn't *mean* to forget it. I won't forget it next time. It's a rotten pan, anyway, to burn itself into a hole jus' for that.'

At this point William's father received a note from a neighbour whose garden adjoined William's and whose life had been rendered intolerable by William's efforts upon his bugle.

The bugle was confiscated.

Darkness descended upon William's soul.

'Well,' he muttered, 'I'm goin' under canvas next week an' I'm jolly *glad* I'm goin'. P'r'aps you'll be sorry when I'm gone.'

He went out into the garden and stood gazing moodily into space, his hands in the pocket of his short scout trousers, for William dressed on any and every occasion in his official costume.

'Can't even have the bugle,' he complained to the landscape. 'Can't even use their rotten ole pans. Can't tie knots in any of their ole things. Wot's the good of *bein'* a scout?'

His indignation grew and with it a desire to be avenged upon his family.

'I'd like to *do* somethin',' he confided to a rose bush with a ferocious scowl. 'Somethin' jus' to show 'em.'

Then his face brightened. He had an idea.

He'd get lost. He'd get really lost. They'd be sorry then all right. They'd p'r'aps think he was dead and they'd be sorry then all right. He imagined their relief, their tearful apologies when at last he returned to the bosom of his family. It was worth trying, anyway.

He set off cheerfully down the drive. He decided to stay away for lunch and supper, and to return at dusk to a penitent, conscience-stricken family.

He first made his way to a neighbouring wood, where he arranged a pile of twigs for a fire, but they refused to light, even with the aid of the match that William found adhering to a piece of putty in the recess of one of his pockets.

Slightly dispirited, he turned his attention to his handkerchief and tied knots in it till it gave way under the strain. William's handkerchiefs, being regularly used to perform the functions of blotting paper among other duties not generally entrusted to handkerchiefs, were always in the last stages of decrepitude.

He felt rather bored and began to wonder whether it was lunchtime or not.

He then 'scouted' the wood and by his woodlore traced

three distinct savage tribes' passage through the wood and found the tracks of several elephants. He engaged in deadly warfare with about half a dozen lions, then tired of the sport. It must be about lunchtime. He could imagine Ethel, his sister, hunting for him wildly high and low with growing pangs of remorse. She'd wish she'd made less fuss over that old scarf. His mother would recall the scene over the pan and her heart would fail her. His father would think with shame of his conduct in the matter of the bugle.

'Poor William! How cruel we were! How different we shall be if only he comes home . . .!'

He could almost hear the words. Perhaps his mother was weeping now. His father – wild-eyed and white-lipped – was pacing his study, waiting for news, eager to atone for his unkindness to his missing son. Perhaps he had the bugle on the table ready to give back to him. Perhaps he'd even bought him a new one.

He imagined the scene of his return. He would be nobly forgiving. He would accept the gift of the new bugle without a word of reproach. His heart thrilled at the thought of it.

He was getting jolly hungry. It must be after lunchtime. But it would spoil it all to go home too early.

Here he caught sight of a minute figure regarding

him with a steady gaze and holding a paper bag in one hand.

William stared down at him.

'Wot you dressed up like that for?' said the apparition, with a touch of scorn in his voice.

William looked down at his sacred uniform and scowled. 'I'm a scout,' he said loftily.

''Cout?' repeated the apparition, with an air of polite boredom. 'Wot's your name?'

'William.'

'Mine's Thomas. Will you catch me a wopse? Look at my wopses!'

He opened the bag slightly and William caught sight of a crowd of wasps buzzing about inside the bag.

'Want more,' demanded the infant. 'Want lots more. Look. Snells!'

He brought out a handful of snails from a miniature pocket, and put them on the ground.

'Watch 'em put their horns out! Watch 'em walk. Look! *They're walkin'*. They're *walkin'*.'

His voice was a scream of ecstasy. He took them up and returned them to their pocket. From another he drew out a wriggling mass.

'Woodlice!' he explained, casually. 'Got worms in 'nother pocket.'

He returned the woodlice to his pocket except one, which he held between a finger and thumb laid thoughtfully against his lip. 'Want wopses now. You get 'em for me.'

William roused himself from his bewilderment.

'How – how do you catch 'em?' he said.

'Wings,' replied Thomas. 'Get hold of their wings an' they don't sting. Sometimes they do, though,' he added casually. 'Then your hands go big.'

A wasp settled near him, and very neatly the young naturalist picked him up and put him in his paper prison.

'Now you get one,' he ordered William.

William determined not to be outshone by this minute but dauntless stranger. As a wasp obligingly settled on a flower near him, he put out his hand, only to withdraw it with a yell of pain and apply it to his mouth.

'Oo – ou!' he said. 'Crumbs!'

Thomas emitted a peal of laughter.

'You stung?' he said. 'Did it sting you? *Funny!*'

William's expression of rage and pain was exquisite to him.

'Come on, boy!' he ordered at last. 'Let's go somewhere else.'

William's bewildered dignity made a last stand.

'*You* can go,' he said. 'I'm playin' by myself.'

'All right!' agreed Thomas. 'You play by you'self an' me play by myself, an' we'll be together – playin' by ourselves.'

He set off down a path, and meekly William followed.

It must be jolly late – almost teatime.

'I'm hungry,' said Thomas suddenly. 'Give me some brekfust.'

'I haven't got any,' said William irritably.

'Well, find some,' persisted the infant.

'I can't. There isn't any to find.'

'Well, buy some!'

'I haven't any money.'

'Well, buy some money.'

Goaded, William turned on him.

'Go away!' he bellowed.

Thomas's blue eyes, beneath a mop of curls, met his coldly.

'Don't talk so loud,' he said sternly. 'There's some blackberries there. You can get me some blackberries.'

William began to walk away, but Thomas trotted by his side.

'There!' he persisted. 'Jus where I'm pointing. Lovely great big suge ones. Get 'em for my brekfust.'

Reluctantly the scout turned to perform his deed of kindness.

Thomas consumed blackberries faster than William could gather them.

'Up there,' he commanded. 'No, the one right up there I want. I want it *kick*. I've etten all the others.'

William was scratched and breathless, and his shirt was torn when at last the rapacious Thomas was satisfied. Then he partook of a little refreshment himself, while Thomas turned out his pockets.

'I'll let 'em go now,' he said.

One of his woodlice, however, stayed motionless where he put it.

'Wot's the matter with it?' said William, curiously.

'I 'speck me's the matter wif it,' said Thomas succinctly. 'Now, get me some lickle fishes, an' tadpoles an' water sings,' he went on cheerfully.

William turned round from his blackberry bush.

'Well, I won't,' he said decidedly. 'I've had enough!'

'You've had 'nuff brekfust,' said Thomas sternly. 'I've found a lickle tin for the sings, so be *kick*. Oo, here's a fly! A green fly! It's sittin' on my finger. Does it like me 'cause it's sittin' on my finger?'

'No,' said William, turning a purple-stained countenance round scornfully.

It must be nearly night. He didn't want to be too hard on them, to make his mother ill or anything. He wanted to be as kind as possible. He'd forgive them at once when he got home. He'd ask for one or two things he wanted, as well as the new bugle. A new penknife, and an engine with a real boiler.

'Waffor does it not like me?' persisted Thomas.

William was silent. Question and questioner were beneath contempt.

'Waffor does it not like me?' he shouted stridently.

'Flies don't like people, silly.'

'Waffor not?' retorted Thomas.

'They don't know anything about them.'

'Well, I'll *tell* it about me. My name's Thomas,' he said to the fly politely. 'Now does it like me?'

William groaned. But the fly had now vanished, and Thomas once more grew impatient.

'Come *on*!' he said. 'Come on an' find sings for me.'

William's manly spirit was by this time so far broken that he followed his new acquaintance to a neighbouring pond, growling threateningly but impotently.

'Now,' commanded his small tyrant, 'take off your boots an' stockings an' go an' find things for me.'

'Take off yours,' growled William, 'an' find things for yourself.'

'No,' said Thomas, 'crockerdiles might be there an'

bite my toes. An pittanopotamuses might be there. If you don't go in, I'll scream an' scream an' *scream*!'

William went in.

He walked gingerly about the muddy pond. Thomas watched him critically from the bank.

'I don't like your *hair*,' he said confidingly.

William growled.

He caught various small swimming objects in the tin, and brought them to the bank for inspection.

'I want more'n that,' said Thomas calmly.

'Well, you won't *get* it,' retorted William.

He began to put on his boots and stockings, wondering desperately how to rid himself of his unwanted companion. But Fate solved the problem. With a loud cry a woman came running down the path.

'Tommy,' she said. 'My little darling Tommy. I thought you were lost!' She turned furiously to William. 'You ought to be ashamed of yourself,' she said. 'A great boy of your age leading a little child like this into mischief! If his father was here, he'd show you. You ought to know better! And you a scout.'

William gasped.

'Well!' he said. 'An' I've bin doin' deeds of kindness on him all morning. I've—'

She turned away indignantly, holding Thomas's hand.

'You're never to go with that nasty rough boy again, darling,' she said.

'Got lots of wopses an' some fishes,' murmured Thomas contentedly.

They disappeared down the path. With a feeling of depression and disillusionment William turned to go home.

SHE TURNED FURIOUSLY TO WILLIAM. 'YOU OUGHT TO BE ASHAMED OF YOURSELF,' SHE SAID.

Then his spirits rose. After all, he'd got rid of Thomas, and he was going home to a contrite family. It must be about supper time. It would be getting dark soon. But it still stayed light a long time now. It wouldn't matter if he just got in for supper. It would have given them time to think things over. He could see his father speaking unsteadily, and holding out his hand.

'My boy . . . let bygones be bygones . . . if there is anything you want . . .'

His father had never said anything of this sort to him yet, but, by a violent stretch of imagination, he could just conceive it.

His mother, of course, would cry over him, and so would Ethel.

'Dear William . . . do forgive us . . . we have been so miserable since you went away . . . we will never treat you so again.'

This again was unlike the Ethel he knew, but sorrow has a refining effect on all characters.

He entered the gate self-consciously. Ethel was at the front door. She looked at his torn shirt and mud-caked knees.

'You'd better hurry if you're going to be ready for lunch,' she said coldly.

'Lunch?' faltered William. 'What time is it?'

'Ten to one. Father's in, so I warn you,' she added unpleasantly.

He entered the house in a dazed fashion. His mother was in the hall.

'*William!*' she said impatiently. 'Another shirt torn! You really are careless. You'll have to stop being a scout if that's the way you treat your clothes. And *look* at your knees!'

Pale and speechless, he went towards the stairs. His father was coming out of the library smoking a pipe. He looked at his son grimly.

'If you aren't downstairs *cleaned* by the time the lunch bell goes, my son,' he said, 'you won't see that bugle of yours this side of Christmas.'

William swallowed.

'Yes, Father,' he said meekly.

He went slowly upstairs to the bathroom.

Life was a rotten show.

CHAPTER 10

THE HELPER

The excitement began at breakfast. William descended slightly late, and, after receiving his parents' reproaches with an air of weary boredom, ate his porridge listlessly. He had come to the conclusion that morning that there was a certain monotonous sameness about life. One got up, and had one's breakfast, and went to school, and had one's dinner, and went to school, and had one's tea, and played, and had one's supper, and went to bed. Even the fact that today was a half-term holiday did not dispel his depression. *One* day's holiday! What good was *one* day? We all have experienced such feelings.

Half-abstractedly he began to listen to his elders' conversation.

'They promised to be here by *nine*,' his mother was saying. 'I do hope they won't be late!'

'Well, it's not much good their coming if the other house isn't ready, is it?' said William's grown-up sister Ethel. 'I don't believe they've even finished *painting*!'

'I'm so sorry it's William's half-term holiday,' sighed Mrs Brown. 'He'll be frightfully in the way.'

'They comin' removin' this *morning*?' he inquired cheerfully.

'Yes, DO try not to hinder them, William.'

'*Me*?' he said indignantly. 'I'm goin' to *help*!'

'If William's going to help,' remarked his father, 'thank heaven *I* shan't be here. Your assistance, William, always seems to be even more devastating in its results than your opposition!'

William smiled politely. Sarcasm was always wasted on William.

'Well,' he said, rising from the table, 'I'd better go an' be gettin' ready to help.'

Ten minutes later Mrs Brown, coming out of the kitchen from her interview with the cook, found to her amazement that the steps of the front door were covered with small ornaments. As she stood staring William appeared from the drawing-room staggering under the weight of a priceless little statuette that had been the property of Mr Brown's great-grandfather.

'WILLIAM!' she gasped.

'I'm gettin' all the little things read for 'em jus' to carry straight down. If I put everything on the steps they don't need come into the house at all. You *said* you didn't want 'em trampin' in dirty boots!'

It took a quarter of an hour to replace them. Over the fragments of a blue Delft bowl Mrs Brown sighed deeply.

'I wish you'd broken *anything* but this, William.'

'Well,' he excused himself, 'you said things *do* get broken removin'. You said so *yourself*! I didn't break it on purpose. It jus' got broken removin'.'

At this point the removers arrived.

There were three of them. One was very fat and jovial, and one was thin and harassed-looking, and a third wore a sheepish smile and walked with a slightly unsteady gait. They made profuse apologies for their lateness.

'You'd better begin with the dining-room,' said Mrs Brown. 'Will you pack the china first? William, get out of the *way*!'

She left them packing, assisted by William. William carried the things to them from the sideboard cupboards.

'What's your names?' he asked, as he stumbled over a glass bowl that he had inadvertently left on the hearth-rug. His progress was further delayed while he conscientiously picked up the fragments. 'Things *do* get broken removin',' he removed.

'Mine is Mister Blake and 'is is Mister Johnson, and 'is is Mister Jones.'

'Which is Mr Jones? The one that walks funny?'

They shook with Herculean laughter, so much so that a china cream jug slipped from Mr Blake's fingers and lay in innumerable pieces round his boots. He kicked them carelessly aside.

'Yus,' he said, bending anew to his task, ''im wot walks funny.'

'Why's he walk funny?' persisted William. 'Has he hurt his legs?'

'Yus,' said Blake with a wink. '' 'E 'urt 'em at the Blue Cow comin' 'ere.'

Mr Jones's sheepish smile broadened into a guffaw.

'Well, you rest,' said William sympathetically. 'You lie down on the sofa an' rest. *I'll* help, so's you needn't do *anything*!'

Mr Jones grew hilarious.

'Come on!' he said. 'My eye! This young gent's all *roight*, 'e is. You lie down an' rest, 'e says! Well, 'ere goes!'

To the huge delight of his companions, he stretched himself at length upon the Chesterfield and closed his eyes. William surveyed him with pleasure.

'That's right,' he said. 'I'll – I'll show you my dog when your legs are better. I've gotter *fine* dog!'

'What sort of a dog?' said Mr Blake, resting from his labours to ask the question.

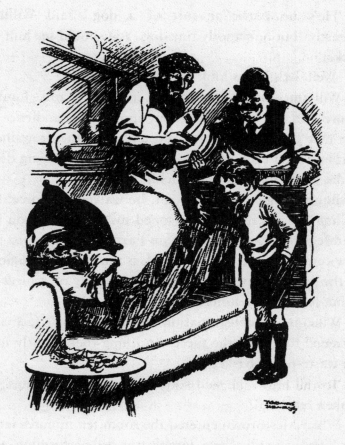

WILLIAM SURVEYED HIM WITH PLEASURE. 'I'LL SHOW YOU
MY DOG WHEN YOUR LEGS ARE BETTER,' HE SAID.

'He's no *partic'lar* sort of a dog,' said William honestly, 'but he's a jolly fine dog. You should see him do tricks!'

'Well, let's 'ave a look at 'im. Fetch 'im art.'

William, highly delighted, complied, and Jumble showed off his best tricks to an appreciative audience of two (Mr Jones had already succumbed to the drowsiness that had long been creeping over him and was lying dead to the world on the Chesterfield).

Jumble begged for a biscuit, he walked (perforce, for William's hand firmly imprisoned his front ones) on his hind legs, he leapt over William's arm. He leapt into the very centre of an old Venetian glass that was on the floor by the packing case and cut his foot slightly on a piece of it, but fortunately suffered no ill effects.

William saw consternation on Mr Johnson's face and hastened to gather the pieces and fling them lightly into the waste-paper basket.

'It's all right,' he said soothingly. 'She *said* things get broken removin'.'

When Mrs Brown entered the room ten minutes later, Mr Jones was still asleep, Jumble was still performing, and Messrs Blake and Johnson were standing in negligent attitudes against the wall appraising the eager Jumble with sportsmanlike eyes.

' 'E's no breed,' Mr Blake was saying, 'but 'e's orl *roight*. I'd loik to see 'im arfter a rat. I bet 'e'd—'

Seeing Mrs Brown, he hastily seized a vase from the mantelpiece and carried it over to the packing case, where he appeared suddenly to be working against time. Mr Johnson followed his example.

Mrs Brown's eyes fell upon Mr Jones and she gasped. 'Whatever—' she began.

' 'E's not very well 'm,' explained Mr Blake obsequiously. ' 'E'll be orl roight when 'e's slep' it orf. 'E's always orl roight when 'e's slep' it orf.'

'He's hurt his legs,' explained William. 'He hurt his legs at the Blue Cow. He's jus' *restin'*!'

Mrs Brown swallowed and counted twenty to herself. It was a practice she had acquired in her youth for use in times when words crowded upon her too thick and fast for utterance.

At last she spoke with unusual bitterness.

'Need he rest with his muddy boots on my Chesterfield?'

At this point Mr Jones awoke from sleep, hypnotised out of it by her cold eyes.

He was profuse in his apologies. He believed he had fainted. He had had a bad headache, brought on probably by exposure to the early morning sun. He felt much better after his faint. He regretted having fainted on to the lady's sofa. He partially brushed off the traces of his dirty boots with an equally dirty hand.

'You've done *nothing* in this room,' said Mrs Brown. 'We shall *never* get finished. William, come away! I'm sure you're hindering them.'

'Me?' said William in righteous indignation. '*Me?* I'm *helpin'*!'

After what seemed to Mrs Brown to be several hours they began on the heavy furniture. They staggered out with the dining-room sideboard, carrying away part of the staircase with it in transit. Mrs Brown, with a paling face, saw her beloved antique cabinet dismembered against the doorpost, and watched her favourite collapsible card table perform a thorough and permanent collapse. Even the hatstand from the hall was devoid of some pegs when it finally reached the van.

'This is simply breaking my heart,' moaned Mrs Brown.

'Where's William?' said Ethel, gloomily, looking round.

'Shh! I don't know. He disappeared a few minutes ago. I don't know *where* he is. I only hope he'll stay there!'

The removers now proceeded to the drawing-room and prepared to take out the piano. They tried it every way.

The first way took a piece out of the doorpost, the second made a dint two inches deep in the piano, the third knocked over the grandfather clock, which fell with a resounding crash, breaking its glass, and incidentally a tall china plant stand that happened to be in its line of descent.

Mrs Brown sat down and covered her face with her hands.

'It's like some dreadful *nightmare*!' she groaned.

Messrs Blake, Johnson and Jones paused to wipe the sweat of honest toil from their brows.

'I dunno *'ow* it's to be got out,' said Mr Blake despairingly.

'It got in!' persisted Mrs Brown. 'If it got in it can get out.'

'We'll 'ave another try,' said Mr Blake with the air of a hero leading a forlorn hope. 'Come on, mites.'

This time was successful and the piano passed safely into the hall, leaving in its wake only a dislocated door handle and a torn chair cover. It then passed slowly and devastatingly down the hall and drive.

The next difficulty was to get it into the van. Messrs Blake, Johnson and Jones tried alone and failed. For ten minutes they tried alone and failed. Between each attempt they paused to mop their brows and throw longing glances towards the Blue Cow, whose signboard was visible down the road.

The gardener, the cook, the housemaid, and Ethel all gave their assistance, and at last, with a superhuman effort, they raised it to the van.

They then all rested weakly against the nearest support and gasped for breath.

'Well,' said Mr Jones, looking reproachfully at the mistress of the house, 'I've never 'andled a pianner—'

At this moment a well-known voice was heard in the recesses of the van, behind the piano and sideboard and hatstand.

'Hey! Let me out! What you've gone blockin' up the van for? I can't get out!'

There was a horror-stricken silence. Then Ethel said sharply:

'What did you go *in* for?'

The mysterious voice came again with a note of irritability.

'Well, I was *restin'*. I mus' have some rest, mustn't I? I've been helpin' all mornin'.'

'Well, couldn't you *see* we were putting things in?'

The unseen presence spoke again.

'No, I can't. I wasn't lookin'!'

'You can't get out, William,' said Mrs Brown desperately. 'We can't move everything again. You must just stop there till it's unpacked. We'll try to push your lunch in to you.'

There was determination in the voice that answered:

'I want to get out! I'm *going* to get out!'

There came tumultuous sounds – the sound of the ripping of some material, of the smashing of glass and of William's voice softly ejaculating 'Crumbs! that ole lookin'-glass gettin' in the way!'

'You'd better take out the piano again,' said Mrs Brown wanly. 'It's the only thing to do.'

With straining, and efforts, and groans, and a certain amount of destruction, the piano was eventually lowered again to the ground. Then the sideboard and hatstand were moved to one side, and finally there emerged from the struggle – William and Jumble. Jumble's coat was covered with little pieces of horsehair, as though from the interior of a chair. William's jersey was torn from shoulder to hem. He looked stern and indignant.

'A nice thing to do!' he began bitterly. 'Shuttin' me up in that ole van. How d'you expect me to breathe, shut in with ole bits of furniture. Folks can't live without air, can they? A nice thing if you'd found me *dead*!'

Emotion had deprived his audience of speech for the time being.

With a certain amount of dignity he walked past them into the house followed by Jumble.

It took another quarter of an hour to replace the piano. As they were making the final effort William came out of the house.

'Here, *I'll* help!' he said, and laid a finger on the side. His presence rather hindered their efforts, but they succeeded in spite of it. William, however, was under the impression that his strength alone had wrought the miracle. He put on an outrageous swagger.

'I'm jolly strong,' he confided to Mr Blake. 'I'm stronger than most folk.'

Here the removers decided that it was time for their midday repast and retired to consume it in the shady back garden. All except Mr Jones, who said he would go down the road for a drink of lemonade. William said that there was lemonade in the larder and offered to fetch it, but Mr Jones said hastily that he wanted a special sort. He had to be very particular what sort of lemonade he drank.

Mrs Brown and Ethel sat down to a scratch meal in the library. William followed his two new friends wistfully into the garden.

'William! Come to lunch!' called Mrs Brown.

'Oh, leave him alone, Mother,' pleaded Ethel. 'Let us have a little peace.'

WILLIAM'S JERSEY WAS TORN FROM SHOULDER TO HEM.
HE LOOKED STERN AND INDIGNANT.

But William did not absent himself for long.

'I want a red handkerchief,' he demanded loudly from the hall.

There was no response.

He appeared in the doorway.

'I say, I want a red handkerchief. Have you gotter red handkerchief, Mother?'

'No, dear.'

'Have you, Ethel?'

'NO!'

'All right,' said William aggrievedly. 'You needn't get mad, need you? I'm only askin' for a red handkerchief. I don't want a red handkerchief off you if you haven't *got* it, do I?'

'William, go *away* and shut the door.'

William obeyed. Peace reigned throughout the house and garden for the next half-hour. Then Mrs Brown's conscience began to prick her.

'William must have something to eat, dear. Do go and find him.'

Ethel went out to the back garden. A scene of happy restfulness met her gaze. Mr Blake reclined against one tree consuming bread and cheese, while a red handkerchief covered his knees. Mr Johnson reclined against another tree, also consuming bread and cheese, while a red handkerchief covered his knees. William leant against a third tree consuming a little heap of scraps collected from the larder, while on his knees also reposed what was apparently a red handkerchief. Jumble sat in the middle catching with nimble, snapping jaws dainties flung to him from time to time by his circle of admirers.

Ethel advanced nearer and inspected William's red handkerchief with dawning horror in her face. Then she gave a scream.

'*William*, that's my silk scarf! It was for a hat. I've only just bought it. Oh, Mother, do *do* something to William! He's taken my new silk scarf – the one I'd got to trim my leghorn. He's the most *awful* boy. I don't think—'

Mrs Brown came out hastily to pacify her. William handed the silk scarf back to its rightful owner.

'Well, I'm *sorry*. I *thought* it was a red handkerchief. It *looked* like a red handkerchief. Well, how could I *know* it wasn't a red handkerchief? I've given it her back. It's all right, Jumble's only bit one end of it. And that's only jam what dropped on it. Well, it'll *wash*, won't it? Well, I've said I'm sorry.

'I don't get much *thanks*,' William continued bitterly. 'Me givin' up my half holiday to helpin' you removin', an' I don't get much *thanks*!'

'Well, William,' said Mrs Brown, 'you can go to the

new house with the first van. He'll be less in the way there,' she confided distractedly to the world in general.

William was delighted with this proposal. At the new house there was a fresh set of men to unload the van, and there was the thrill of making their acquaintance.

Then the front gate was only just painted and bore a notice 'Wet Paint'. It was, of course, incumbent upon William to test personally the wetness of the paint. His trousers bore testimony to the testing to their last day, in spite of many applications of turpentine. Jumble also tested it, and had in fact to be disconnected from the front gate by means of a pair of scissors. For many weeks the first thing that visitors to the Brown household saw was a little tuft of Jumble's hair adorning the front gate.

William then proceeded to 'help' to the utmost of his power. He stumbled up from the van to the house staggering under the weight of a medicine cupboard, and leaving a trail of broken bottles and little pools of medicine behind. Jumble sampled many of the latter and became somewhat thoughtful.

It was found that the door of a small bedroom at the top of the stairs was locked, and this fact (added to Mr Jones's failure to return from his lemonade) rather impeded the progress of the unpackers.

'Brike it open,' suggested one.

'Better not.'

'Per'aps the key's insoide,' suggested another brightly.

William had one of his brilliant ideas.

'Tell you what I'll do,' he said eagerly and importantly. 'I'll climb up to the roof an' get down the chimney an' open it from the inside.'

They greeted the proposal with guffaws.

They did not know William.

It was growing dusk when Mrs Brown and Ethel and the second van load appeared.

'What is that on the gate?' said Ethel, stooping to examine the part of Jumble's coat that brightened up the dullness of the black paint.

'It's that *dog*!' said Mrs Brown.

Then came a ghostlike cry, apparently from the heavens.

'Mother!'

Mrs Brown raised a startled countenance to the skies. There seemed to be nothing in the skies that could have addressed her.

Then she suddenly saw a small face peering down over the coping of the roof. It was a face that was very frightened, under a superficial covering of soot. It was William's face.

'I can't get down,' it said hoarsely.

Mrs Brown's heart stood still.

'Stay where you are, William,' she said faintly. 'Don't *move*.'

The entire staff of removers was summoned. A ladder was borrowed from a neighbouring garden and found to be too short. Another was fetched and fastened to it. William, at his dizzy height, was growing irritable.

'I can't stay up here for *ever*,' he said severely.

At last he was rescued by his friend Mr Blake and brought down to safety. His account was confused.

'I wanted to *help*. I wanted to open that door for 'em, so I climbed up by the scullery roof, an' the ivy, an' the drainpipe, an' I tried to get down the chimney. I didn't know which one it was, but I tried 'em all an' they were all too little, an' I tried to get down by the ivy again but I couldn't, so I waited till you came an' hollered out. I wasn't scared,' he said, fixing them with a stern eye. 'I wasn't scared a bit. I jus' wanted to get down. An' this ole black chimney stuff tastes beastly. No, I'm all right,' he ended, in answer to tender inquiries. 'I'll go on helpin'.'

He was with difficulty persuaded to retire to bed at a slightly earlier hour than usual.

'Well,' he confessed, 'I'm a bit tired with helpin' all day.'

Soon after he had gone Mr Brown and Robert arrived.

The Helper

'And how have things gone today?' said Mr Brown cheerfully.

'Thank heaven William goes to school tomorrow,' said Ethel devoutly.

Upstairs in his room William was studying himself in the glass – torn jersey, paint-stained trousers, blackened face.

'Well,' he said with a deep sigh of satisfaction, 'I guess I've jolly well HELPED today!'

CHAPTER 11

WILLIAM AND THE SMUGGLER

William's family were going to the seaside for February. It was not an ideal month for the seaside, but William's father's doctor had ordered him a complete rest and change.

'We shall have to take William with us, you know,' his wife had said as they discussed plans.

'Good heavens!' groaned Mr Brown. 'I thought it was to be a *rest* cure.'

'Yes, but you know what he is,' his wife urged. 'I daren't leave him with anyone. Certainly not with Ethel. We shall have to take them both. Ethel will help with him.'

Ethel was William's grown-up sister.

'All right,' agreed her husband finally. 'You can take all responsibility. I formally disown him from now till we get back. I don't care *what* trouble he lands you in. You know what he is and you deliberately take him away with me on a rest cure!'

'It can't be helped, dear,' said his wife mildly.

William was thrilled by the news. It was several years since he had been at the seaside.

'Will I be able to go swimmin'?'

'It *won't* be too cold! Well, if I wrap up warm, will I be able to go swimmin'?'

'Can I catch fishes?'

'Are there lots of smugglers smugglin' there?'

'Well, I'm only *askin'*, you needn't get mad!'

One afternoon Mrs Brown missed her best silver tray and searched the house high and low for it wildly, while dark suspicions of each servant in turn arose in her usually unsuspicious breast.

It was finally discovered in the garden. William had dug a large hole in one of the garden beds. Into the bottom of this he had fitted the tray and had lined the sides with bricks. He had then filled it with water and taking off his shoes and stockings stepped up and down his narrow pool. He was distinctly aggrieved by Mrs Brown's reproaches.

'Well, I was practisin' paddlin', ready for goin' to the seaside. I didn't *mean* to rune your tray. You talk as if I *meant* to rune your tray. I was only practisin' paddlin'.'

At last the day of departure arrived. William was instructed to put his things ready on his bed, and his mother would then come and pack for him. He summoned her proudly over the balusters after about twenty minutes.

'I've got everythin' ready, Mother.'

Mrs Brown ascended to his room.

Upon his bed was a large popgun, a football, a dormouse in a cage, a punchball on a stand, a large box of 'curios', and a buckskin which was his dearest possession and had been presented to him by an uncle from South Africa.

Mrs Brown sat down weakly on a chair.

'You can't possibly take any of these things,' she said faintly but firmly.

'Well, you *said* put my things on the bed for you to pack an' I've put them on the bed, an' now you say—'

'I meant clothes.'

'Oh, *clothes*!' he said scornfully. 'I never thought of *clothes*.'

'Well, you can't take any of these things, anyway.'

William hastily began to defend his collection of treasures.

'I *mus*' have the popgun 'cause you never know. There may be pirates an' smugglers down there, an' you can *kill* a man with a popgun if you get near enough and know the right place, an' I might need it. An' I *must* have the foot-

ball to play on the sands with, an' the punchball to prac-
tise boxin' on, an' I *must* have the dormouse, 'cause –
'cause to feed him, an' I *must* have this box of things and
this skin to show to folks I meet down at the seaside 'cause
they're int'restin'.'

But Mrs Brown was firm, and William reluctantly
yielded.

In a moment of weakness, finding that his trunk was
only three quarters filled by his things, she slipped in his
beloved buckskin, while William himself put the popgun
inside when no one was looking.

They had been unable to obtain a furnished house, so
had to be content with a boarding house. Mr Brown was
eloquent on the subject.

'If you're deliberately turning that child loose into a
boarding house full, presumably, of quiet, inoffensive
people, you deserve all you get. It's nothing to do with me.
I'm going to have a rest cure. I've disowned him. He can
do as he likes.'

'It can't be helped, dear,' said Mrs Brown mildly.

Mr Brown had engaged one of the huts on the beach
chiefly for William's use, and William proudly furnished
its floor with the buckskin.

'It was killed by my uncle,' he announced to the small
crowd of children at the door who had watched with

interest his painstaking measuring on the floor in order to place his treasure in the exact centre. 'He killed it dead – jus' like this.'

William had never heard the story of the death of the buck, and therefore had invented one in which he had gradually come to confuse himself with his uncle in the role of hero.

'It was walkin' about an' I – he – met it. I hadn't got no gun, and it sprung at me an' I caught hold of its neck with one hand an' I broke off its horns with the other, an' I knocked it over. An' it got up an' ran at me – him – again, an' I jus' tripped it up with my foot an' it fell over again, an' then I jus' give it one big hit with my fist right on its head, an' it killed it an' it died!'

There was an incredulous gasp.

Then there came a clear, high voice from behind the crowd.

'Little boy, you are not telling the truth.'

William looked up into a thin, spectacled face.

'I wasn't tellin' it to you,' he remarked, wholly unabashed.

A little girl with dark curls took up the cudgels quite needlessly in William's defence.

'He's a very *brave* boy to do all that,' she said indignantly. 'So don't you go *saying* things to him.'

'Well,' said William, flattered but modest, 'I didn't say I did, did I? I said my uncle – well, partly my uncle.'

Mr Percival Jones looked down at him in righteous wrath.

'You're a very wicked little boy. I'll tell your father – er – I'll tell your sister.'

For Ethel was approaching in the distance and Mr Percival Jones was in no way loath to converse with her.

Mr Percival Jones was a thin, pale, aesthetic would-be poet who lived and thrived on the admiration of the elderly ladies of his boarding house, and had done so for the past ten years. Once he had published a volume of poems at his own expense. He lived at the same boarding house as the Browns, and had seen Ethel in the distance at meals. He had admired the red lights in her dark hair and the blue of her eyes, and had even gone so far as to wonder whether she possessed the solid and enduring qualities which he would require of one whom in his mind he referred to as his 'future spouse'.

He began to walk down the beach with her.

'I should like to speak to you – er – about your brother, Miss Brown,' he began, 'if you can spare me the time, of course. I trust I do not er – intrude or presume. He is a charming little man but – er – I fear – not veracious. May I accompany you a little on your way? I am – er –

much attracted to your – er – family. I – er – should like to know you all better. I am – er – deeply attached to your – er – little brother, but grieved to find that he does not – er – adhere to the truth in his statements. I – er—'

Miss Brown's blue eyes were dancing with merriment.

'Oh, don't worry about William,' she said. 'He's *awful*. It's much better just to leave him alone. Isn't the sea gorgeous today?'

They walked along the sands.

Meanwhile William had invited his small defender into his hut.

'You can look round,' he said graciously. 'You've seen my skin what I – he – killed, haven't you? This is my gun. You put a cork in there and it comes out hard when you shoot it. It would kill anyone,' he said impressively, 'if you did it near enough to them and at the right place. An' I've got a dormouse, an' a punchball, an' a box of things, an' a football, but they wouldn't let me bring them,' bitterly.

'It's a *lovely* skin,' said the little girl. 'What's your name?'

'William. What's yours?'

'Peggy.'

'Well, let's be on a desert island, shall we? An' nothin' to eat nor anything, shall we? Come on.'

She nodded eagerly.

'How *lovely*!'

They wandered out on to the promenade, and among a large crowd of passers-by bemoaned the lonely emptiness of the island and scanned the horizon for a sail. In the far distance on the cliffs could be seen the figures of Mr

'YOU'RE A VERY WICKED LITTLE BOY!' SAID MR PERCIVAL
JONES.

Percival Jones and William's sister, walking slowly away from the town.

At last they turned towards the hut.

'We must find somethin' to eat,' said William firmly. 'We can't let ourselves starve to death.'

'Shrimps?' suggested Peggy cheerfully.

'We haven't got nets,' said William. 'We couldn't save them from the wreck.'

'Periwinkles?'

'There aren't any on this island. I know! Seaweed! An' we'll cook it.'

'Oh, how *lovely*!'

He gathered up a handful of seaweed and they entered the hut, leaving a white handkerchief tied on to the door to attract the attention of any passing ship. The hut was provided with a gas ring and William, disregarding his family's express injunction, lit this and put on a saucepan filled with water and seaweed.

'We'll pretend it's a wood fire,' he said. 'We couldn't make a real wood fire out on the prom. They'd stop us. So we'll pretend this is. An' we'll pretend we saved a saucepan from the wreck.'

After a few minutes he took off the pan and drew out a long green strand.

'You eat it first,' he said politely.

The smell of it was not pleasant. Peggy drew back.

'Oh, no, you first!'

'No, you,' said William nobly. 'You look hungrier than me.'

She bit off a piece, chewed it, shut her eyes and swallowed.

'Now you,' she said with a shade of vindictiveness in her voice. 'You're not going to not have any.'

William took a mouthful and shivered.

'I think it's gone bad,' he said critically.

Peggy's rosy face had paled.

'I'm going home,' she said suddenly.

'You can't go home on a desert island,' said William severely.

'Well, I'm going to be rescued then,' she said.

'I think I am, too,' said William.

It was lunchtime when William arrived at the boarding house. Mr Percival Jones had moved his place so as to be nearer Ethel. He was now convinced that she was possessed of every virtue his future 'spouse' could need. He conversed brightly and incessantly during the meal. Mr Brown grew restive.

'The man will drive me mad,' he said afterwards. 'Bleating away! What's he bleating about anyway? Can't you stop him bleating, Ethel? You seem to have influence.

Bleat! Bleat! Bleat! Good Lord! And me here for a *rest* cure.'

At this point he was summoned to the telephone and returned distraught.

'It's an unknown female,' he said. 'She says that a boy of the name of William from this boarding house has made her little girl sick by forcing her to eat seaweed. She says its brutal. Does anyone *know* I'm here for a rest cure? Where is the boy? Good heavens! Where is the boy?'

But William, like Peggy, had retired from the world for a space. He returned later on in the afternoon, looking pale and chastened. He bore the reproaches of his family in stately silence.

Mr Percival Jones was in great evidence in the drawing-room.

'And soon – er – soon the – er – spring will be with us once more,' he was saying in his high-pitched voice as he leant back in his chair and joined the tips of his fingers together. 'The spring – ah – the spring! I have a – er – little effort I – er – composed on – er – the Coming of Spring – I – er – will read to you sometime if you will – ah – be kind enough to – er – criticise – ah – impartially.'

'*Criticise!*' they chorused. 'It will be above criticism. Oh, do read it to us, Mr Jones.'

'I will – er – this evening.' His eyes wandered to the

door, hoping and longing for his beloved's entrance. But Ethel was with her father at a matinee at the Winter Gardens and he looked and longed in vain. In spite of this, however, the springs of his eloquence did not run dry, and he held forth ceaselessly to his little circle of admirers.

'The simple – ah – pleasures of nature. How few of us – alas! – have the – er – gift of appreciating them rightly. This – er – little seaside hamlet with its – er – sea, its – er – promenade, its – er – Winter Gardens! How beautiful it is! How few appreciate it rightly!'

Here William entered and Mr Percival Jones broke off abruptly. He disliked William.

'Ah! Here comes our little friend. He looks pale. Remorse, my young friend? Ah, beware of untruthfulness. Beware of the beginnings of a life of lies and deception.' He laid a hand on William's head and cold shivers ran down William's spine. ' "Be good, sweet child, and let who will be clever," as the poet says.' There was murder in William's heart.

At that minute Ethel entered.

'No,' she snapped. 'I sat next to a man who smelt of bad tobacco. I *hate* men who smoke bad tobacco.'

Mr Jones assumed an expression of intense piety.

'I may boast,' he said sanctimoniously, 'that I have never thus soiled my lips with drink or smoke . . .'

There was an approving murmur from the occupants of the drawing-room.

William had met his father in the passage outside the drawing-room. Mr Brown was wearing a hunted expression.

'Can I go into the drawing-room,' he said bitterly, 'or is he bleating away in there?'

They listened. From the drawing-room came the sound of a high-pitched voice.

Mr Brown groaned.

'Good Lord!' he moaned. 'And I'm here for a *rest* cure and he comes bleating into every room in the house. Is the smoking-room safe? Does he smoke?'

Mr Percival Jones was feeling slightly troubled in his usually peaceful conscience. He could honestly say that he had never smoked. He could honestly say that he had never drunk. But in his bedroom reposed two bottles of brandy, purchased at the advice of an aunt 'in case of emergencies'. In his bedroom also was a box of cigars that he had bought for a cousin's birthday gift, but which his conscience had finally forbidden to present. He decided to consign these two emblems of vice to the waves that very evening.

Meanwhile William had returned to the hut and was composing a tale of smugglers by the light of a candle. He was much intrigued by his subject. He wrote fast in an illegible hand in great sloping lines, his brows frowning, his tongue protruding from his mouth as it always did in moments of mental strain.

His sympathies wavered between the smugglers and the representatives of law and order. His orthography was the despair of his teachers.

'"*Ho!*" *sez Dick Savage,*' he wrote. '"*Ho! Gadzooks! Rol in the bottles of beer up the beach. Fill your pockets with the baccy from the bote. Quick, now! Gadzooks! Methinks we are observed!*" *He glared round in the darkness. In less time than wot it takes to rite this he was srounded by pleesemen and stood, proud and defiant, in the light of there electrick torches wot they had wiped quick as litening from their busums.*

'"*Surrender!*" *cried one, holding a gun at his brain and a drorn sord at his hart, "Surrender or die!*"

'"*Never,*" *said Dick Savage, throwing back his head, proud and defiant. "Never. Do to me wot you will I die.*"

'*One crule brute hit him a blo on the lips and he sprang back, snarling with rage. In less time than wot it takes to rite this he had sprang at his torturer's throte and his teeth met in one mighty bite. His torturer dropped ded and lifless at his feet.*

'"*Ho!*" *cried Dick Savage, throwing back his head,*

proud and defiant again. "So dies any of you wot insults my proud manhood. I will meet my teeth in your throtes."

'*For a minit they stood trembling, then one, bolder than the rest, lept forward and tide Dick Savage's hands with rope behind his back. Another took from his pockets bottles of beer and tobacco in large quantities.*

'*"Ho!" they cried exulting. "Ho! Dick Savage the smugler caught at last!"*

'*Dick Savage gave one proud and defiant laugh, and, bringing his tide hands over his hed he bit the rope with one mighty bite.*

'*"Ho! Ho!" he cried, throwing back his proud hed. "Ho, ho! You dirty dogs!"*

'*Then, draining to the dregs a large bottle of poison he had concealed in his busum he fell ded and lifless at there feet.*'

There was a timid knock at the door and William, scowling impatiently, rose to open it.

'What d'you want?' he said curtly.

A little voice answered from the dusk.

'It's me – Peggy. I've come to se how you are, William. They don't know I've come. I was awful sick after that seaweed this morning, William.'

William looked at her with a superior frown.

'Go away,' he said. 'I'm busy.'

'What are you doing?' she said, poking her little curly head into the doorway.

'I'm writin' a tale.'

She clasped her hands.

'Oh, how lovely! Oh, William, do read it to me. I'd *love* it!'

Mollified, he opened the door and she took her seat on his buckskin on the floor, and William sat by the candle, clearing his throat for a minute before he began. During the reading she never took her eyes off him. At the end she drew a deep breath.

'Oh, William, it's beautiful. William, are there smugglers now?'

'Oh, yes. Millions,' he said carelessly.

'*Here?*'

'Of course there are!'

She went to the door and looked out at the dusk.

'I'd love to see one. What do they smuggle, William?'

He came and joined her at the door, walking with a slight swagger as became a man of literary fame.

'Oh, beer an' cigars an' things. *Millions* of them.'

A furtive figure was passing the door, casting suspicious glances to left and right. He held his coat tightly round him, clasping something inside it.

'I expect that's one,' said William casually.

They watched the figure out of sight.

Suddenly William's eyes shone.

'Let's stalk him an' catch him,' he said excitedly. 'Come on. Let's take some weapons.' He seized his popgun from a corner. 'You take' – he looked round the room – 'you take the waste-paper basket to put over his head an' – an' pin down his arms an' somethin' to tie him up! – I know – the skin I – he – shot in Africa. You can tie its paws in front of him. Come on! Let's catch him smugglin'.'

He stepped out boldly into the dusk with his popgun, followed by the blindly obedient Peggy carrying the waste-paper basket in one hand and the skin in the other.

Mr Percival Jones was making quite a little ceremony of consigning his brandy and cigars to the waves. He had composed 'a little effort' upon it which began,

> *O deeps, receive these objects vile*
> *Which nevermore mine eyes shall soil.*

He went down to the edge of the sea and, taking a bottle in hand, held them out at arms' length, while he began in his high-pitched voice,

> *O deeps, receive these—*

He stopped. A small boy stood beside him holding out at him the point of what in the semi-darkness Mr Jones took to be a loaded rifle. William mistook his action in holding out the bottles.

'It's no good tryin' to drink it up,' he said severely. 'We've caught you smugglin'.'

Mr Percival Jones laughed nervously.

'My little man!' he said. 'That's a very dangerous – er

'WE'VE CAUGHT YOU SMUGGLIN'!' WILLIAM
SAID SEVERELY.

195

– thing for you to have! Suppose you hand it over to me, now, like a good little chap.'

William recognised his voice.

'Fancy you bein' a smuggler all the time!' he said with righteous indignation in his voice.

'Take away that – er – nasty gun, little boy,' pleaded his captive plaintively. 'You – ah – don't understand it. It – er – might go off.'

William was not a boy to indulge in half measures. He meant to carry the matter off with a high hand.

'I'll shoot you dead,' he said dramatically, 'if you don't do jus' what I tell you.'

Mr Percival Jones wiped the perspiration from his brow.

'Where did you get that rifle, little boy?' he asked in a voice he strove to make playful. 'Is it – ah – is it loaded? It's – ah – unwise, little boy. Most unwise. Er – give it to me to – er – take care of. It – er – might go off, you know.'

William moved the muzzle of his weapon, and Mr Percival Jones shuddered from head to foot. William was a brave boy, but he had experienced a moment of cold terror when first he had approached his captive. The first note of the quavering high-pitched voice had, however, reassured him. He instantly knew himself to be the better man. His captive's obvious terror of his popgun almost persuaded him that he held in his hand some formidable death-dealing instrument. As a matter of fact Mr Percival Jones was temperamentally an abject coward.

'You walk up to the seats,' commanded William. 'I've took you prisoner for smugglin' an' – an' – jus' walk up to the seats.'

Mr Percival Jones obeyed with alacrity.

'Don't – er – *press* anything, little boy,' he pleaded as he went. 'It – ah – might go off by accident. You might do – ah – untold damage.'

Peggy, armed with the waste-paper basket and the skin, followed open-mouthed.

At the seat William paused.

'Peggy, you put the basket over his head an' pin his arms down – case he struggles, an' tie the skin wot I shot round him, case he struggles.'

Peggy stood upon the seat and obeyed. Their victim made no protest. He seemed to himself to be in some horrible dream. The only thing of which he was conscious was the dimly descried weapon that William held out at him in the darkness. He was hardly aware of the waste-paper basket thrust over his head. He watched William anxiously through the basketwork.

'Be careful,' he murmured. 'Be careful, boy!'

He hardly felt the skin which was fastened tightly

round his unresisting form by Peggy, the tail tied to one front paw. Unconsciously he still clasped a bottle of brandy in each arm.

Then came the irate summons of Peggy's nurse through the dusk.

'Oh, William,' she said panting with excitement, 'I don't want to leave you. Oh, William, he might *kill* you!'

'You go on. I'm all right,' he said with conscious valour. 'He can't do nothin' 'cause I've got a gun an' I can shoot him dead' – Mr Percival Jones shuddered afresh – 'an' he's all tied up an' I've took him prisoner an' I'm goin' to take him home.'

'Oh, William, you *are* brave!' she whispered in the darkness as she flitted away to her nurse.

William blushed with pride and embarrassment.

Mr Percival Jones was convinced that he had to deal with a youthful lunatic, armed with a dangerous weapon, and was anxious only to humour him till the time of danger was over and he could be placed under proper restraint.

Unconscious of his peculiar appearance, he walked before his captor, casting propitiatory glances behind him.

'It's all right, little boy,' he said soothingly, 'quite all right. I'm – er – your friend. Don't – ah – get annoyed, little boy. Don't – ah – get annoyed. Won't you put your – gun down, little man? Won't you let me carry it for you?'

William walked behind still pointing his popgun.

'I've took you prisoner for smugglin',' he repeated doggedly. 'I'm takin' you home. You're my prisoner. I've took you.'

They met no one on the road, though Mr Percival Jones threw longing glances around, ready to appeal to any passer-by for rescue. He was afraid to raise his voice in case it should rouse his youthful captor to murder. He saw with joy the gate of his boarding house and hastened up the walk and up the stairs. The drawing-room door was open. There was help and assistance, there was protection against this strange persecution. He entered, followed closely by William. It was about the time he had promised to read his 'little effort' on the Coming of Spring to his circle of admirers. A group of elderly ladies sat round the fire awaiting him. Ethel was writing. They turned as he entered and a gasp of horror and incredulous dismay went up. It was that gasp that called him to a realisation of the fact that he was wearing a waste-paper basket over his head and shoulders, and that a mangy fur was tied round his arms.

'Mr *Jones*!' they gasped.

He gave a wrench to his shoulders and the rug fell to

the floor, revealing a bottle of brandy clasped in either arm.

'Mr *Jones*!' they repeated.

'I caught him smugglin',' said William proudly. 'I caught him smugglin' beer by the sea an' he was drinking those two bottles he'd smuggled an' he had thousands an' *thousands* of cigars all over him, an' I caught him, an' he's a smuggler, an' I brought him up here with my gun. He's a smuggler an' I took him prisoner.'

Mr Jones, red and angry, his hair awry, glared through the wickerwork of the basket. He moistened his lips. 'This is an outrage,' he spluttered.

Horrified elderly eyes stared at the incriminating bottles.

'He was drinkin' 'em by the sea,' said William.

'Mr *Jones*!' they chorused again.

He flung off his waste-paper basket and turned upon the proprietress of the establishment who stood by the door.

'I will not brook such treatment,' he stammered in fury. 'I leave your roof tonight. I am outraged – humiliated. I – I disdain to explain. I – leave your roof tonight.'

'Mr *Jones*!' they said once more.

Mr Jones, still clasping his bottles, withdrew, pausing to glare at William on his way.

'You *wicked* boy! You *wicked* little, *untruthful* boy,' he said.

William looked after him. 'He's my prisoner an' they've let him go,' he said aggrievedly.

Ten minutes later he wandered into the smoking-room. Mr Brown sat miserably in a chair by a dying fire beneath a poor light.

'Is he still bleating there?' he said. 'Is this still the only

'I CAUGHT HIM SMUGGLIN',' WILLIAM EXPLAINED PROUDLY.
'HE HAD THOUSANDS AN' THOUSANDS OF CIGARS AND
THAT BEER!'

corner where I can be sure of keeping my sanity? Is he reading his beastly poetry upstairs? Is he—'

'He's goin',' said William moodily. 'He's goin' before dinner. They've sent for his cab. He's mad 'cause I said he was a smuggler. He was a smuggler 'cause I saw him doin' it, an' I took him prisoner an' he got mad an' he's goin'. An' they're mad at me 'cause I took him prisoner. You'd think they'd be glad at me catchin' smugglers, but they're not,' bitterly. 'An' Mother says she'll tell you an' you'll be mad too an'—'

Mr Brown raised his hand.

'One minute, my son,' he said. 'Your story is confused. Do I understand that Mr Jones is going and that you are the cause of his departure?'

'Yes, 'cause he got mad 'cause I said he was a smuggler an' he was a smuggler an' they're mad at me now, an'—'

Mr Brown laid a hand on his son's shoulder.

'There are moments, William,' he said, 'when I feel almost affectionate towards you.'

CHAPTER 12

THE REFORM OF WILLIAM

To William the idea of reform was new and startling and not wholly unattractive. It originated with the housemaid whose brother was a reformed burglar now employed in a grocer's shop.

''E's got conversion,' she said to William. ''E got it quite sudden, like, an' 'e give up all 'is bad ways straight off. 'E's bin like a heavenly saint ever since.'

William was deeply interested. The point was all innocently driven in later by the Sunday-school mistress. William's family had no real faith in the Sunday school as a corrective to William's inherent wickedness, but they knew that no Sabbath peace or calm was humanly possible while William was in the house. So they brushed and cleaned and tidied him at 2.45 and sent him, pained and protesting, down the road every Sunday afternoon. Their only regret was that Sunday school did not begin earlier and end later.

Fortunately for William, most of his friends' parents were inspired by the same zeal, so that he met his old cronies of the weekdays – Henry, Ginger, Douglas and all the rest – and together they beguiled the monotony of the Sabbath.

But this Sunday the tall, pale lady who, for her sins, essayed to lead William and his friends along the straight and narrow path of virtue, was almost inspired. She was like some prophetess of old. She was so emphatic that the red cherries that hung coquettishly over the edge of her hat rattled against it as though in applause.

'We must all *start afresh*,' she said. 'We must all be *turned* – that's what *conversion* means.'

William's fascinated eye wandered from the cherries to the distant view out of the window. He thought suddenly of the noble burglar who had turned his back upon the mysterious, nefarious tools of his trade and now dispensed margarine to his former victims.

Opposite him sat a small girl in a pink and white checked frock. He often whiled away the dullest hours of Sunday school by putting out his tongue at her or throwing paper pellets at her (manufactured previously for the purpose). But today, meeting her serious eye, he looked away hastily.

'And we must all *help someone*,' went on the urgent voice. 'If we have *turned* ourselves, we must help someone else to *turn* . . .'

Determined and eager was the eye that the small girl turned upon William, and William realised that his time had come. He was to be converted. He felt almost thrilled by the prospect. He was so enthralled that he received absent-mindedly, and without gratitude, the mountainous bull's eye passed to him from Ginger, and only gave a half-hearted smile when a well-aimed pellet from Henry's hand sent one of the prophetess's cherries swinging high in the air.

After the class the pink-checked girl (whose name most appropriately was Deborah) stalked William for several yards and finally cornered him.

'William,' she said, 'are you going to *turn*?'

'I'm goin' to think about it,' said William guardedly.

'William, I think you ought to turn. I'll help you,' she added sweetly.

William drew a deep breath. 'All right, I will,' he said.

She heaved a sigh of relief.

'You'll begin *now*, won't you?' she said earnestly.

William considered. There were several things that he had wanted to do for some time, but hadn't managed to do yet. He had not tried turning off the water at the main, and hiding the key and seeing what would happen; he hadn't tried shutting up the cat in the hen house; he hadn't tried painting his long-suffering mongrel Jumble with the pot of green paint that was in the tool shed; he hadn't tried pouring water into the receiver of the telephone; he hadn't tried locking the cook into the larder. There were, in short, whole fields of crime entirely unexplored. All these things – and others – must be done before the reformation.

'I can't begin *jus'* yet,' said William. 'Say day after to-morrow.'

She considered this for a minute.

'Very well,' she said at last reluctantly, 'day after to-morrow.'

The next day dawned bright and fair. William arose with a distinct sense that something important had happened. Then he thought of the reformation. He saw himself leading a quiet and blameless life, walking sedately to school, working at high pressure in school, doing his homework conscientiously in the evening, being exquisitely polite to his family, his instructors, and the various foolish people who visited his home for the sole purpose (apparently) of making inane remarks to him. He saw all this, and the picture was far from unattractive – in the distance. In the immediate future, however, there were various quite important things to be done. There was a whole normal lifetime of crime to be crowded into one day. Looking out of his window he espied the gardener bending over one of the beds. The gardener had a perfectly bald head. William had sometimes idly imagined the impact of a pea sent violently from a pea-shooter at the gardener's bald head. Before there had been a lifetime of experiment before him, and he had put off this one idly in favour of something more pressing. Now there was only one day. He took up his pea-shooter and aimed carefully. The pea did not embed itself deeply into the gardener's skull as William had sometimes thought it would. It bounced back. It bounced back quite hard. The gardener also bounced back with a yell of anger, shaking his fist at William's window. But William had discreetly retired. He hid the pea-shooter, assumed his famous expression of innocence, and felt distinctly cheered. The question as to what exactly would happen when the pea met the baldness was now for ever solved. The gardener retired grumbling to the potting shed, so, for the present, all was well. Later in the day the gardener might lay his formal complaint before authority, but later in the day was later in the day. It did not trouble William. He dressed briskly and went down to breakfast with a frown of concentration upon his face. It was the last day of his old life.

No one else was in the dining-room. It was the work of a few minutes to remove the bacon from beneath the big

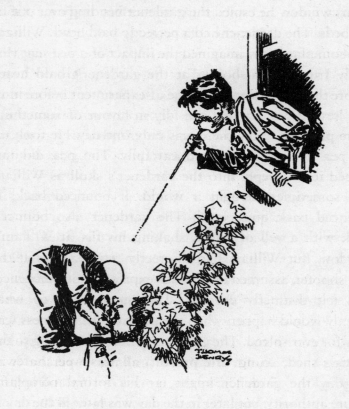

THE PEA DID NOT EMBED ITSELF INTO THE GARDENER'S
SKULL AS WILLIAM HAD SOMETIMES THOUGHT IT
WOULD. IT BOUNCED BACK. THE GARDENER ALSO
BOUNCED BACK.

pewter cover and substitute the kitten, to put a table-spoonful of salt into the coffee, and to put a two-day's-old paper in place of that morning's. They were all things that he had at one time or another vaguely thought of doing, but for which he had never yet seemed to have time or opportunity. Warming to his subject he removed the egg from under the egg cosy on his sister's plate and placed in its stead a worm which had just appeared in the window box in readiness for the early bird.

He surveyed the scene with a deep sigh of satisfaction. The only drawback was that he felt that he could not safely stay to watch results. William possessed a true strategic instinct for the right moment for a retreat. Hearing, therefore, a heavy step on the stairs, he seized several pieces of toast and fled. As he fled he heard through the open window violent sounds proceeding from the enraged kitten beneath the cover, and then the still more violent sounds proceeding from the unknown person who removed the cover. The kitten, a mass of fury and lust for revenge, came flying through the window. William hid behind a laurel bush till it had passed, then set off down the road. School, of course, was impossible. The precious hours of such a day as this could not be wasted in school. He went down the road full of his whole purpose. The wickedness of a lifetime was somehow or other to be crowded into this day. Tomorrow it would all be impossible. Tomorrow began the blameless life. It must all be worked off today. He skirted the school by a field path in case any of those narrow souls paid to employ so aimlessly the precious hours of his youth might be there. They would certainly be tactless enough to question him as he passed the door. Then he joined the main road. The main road was empty except for a caravan – a caravan gaily painted in red and yellow. It had little lace curtains at the window. It was altogether a most fascinating caravan. No one seemed to be near it. William looked through the window. There was a kind of dresser with crockery hanging from it, a small table and a little oil stove. The further part was curtained off but no sound came from it, so that it was presumably empty too. William wandered round to inspect the quadruped in front. It appeared to be a mule – a mule with a jaundiced view of life. It rolled a sad eye towards William, then with a deep sigh returned to its contemplation of the landscape. William gazed upon caravan and steed fascinated. Never, in his future life of noble merit, would he be able to annex a caravan. It was his last chance. No one was about. He could pretend that he had mistaken it for his own caravan or had got on to it by mistake or – or anything. Conscience stirred faintly in his breast, but he silenced it sternly. Conscience was to rule him for the rest of his life and it could jolly well let him alone *this* day. With some difficulty he climbed on to the driver's seat, took the reins, said 'Gee up' to the melancholy mule, and the whole equipage with a jolt and faint rattle set out along the road. William did not know how to drive, but it did not seem to matter. The mule ambled along and William, high up on the driver's seat, the reins held with ostentatious carelessness in one hand, the whip poised lightly in the other, was in the seventh heaven of bliss. He was driving a caravan. He was driving a caravan. He was driving a caravan. The very telegraph posts seemed to gape with envy and admiration as he passed. What ultimately he was going to do with his caravan he neither knew nor cared. All that mattered was, it was a bright sunny morning, and all the others were in school, and he was driving a red and yellow caravan along the high road. The birds seemed to be singing a paeon of praise to him. He was intoxicated with pride. It was *his* caravan, *his* road, *his* world. Carelessly he flicked the mule with the whip. There are several explanations of what happened then. The mule may not have been used to the whip; a wasp may have just stung him at that particular minute; a wandering demon may have entered into him. Mules are notoriously accessible to wandering demons. Whatever the explanation, the mule suddenly started

forward and galloped at full speed down the hill. The reins
dropped from William's hands; he clung for dear life on to
his seat, as the caravan, swaying and jolting along the
uneven road, seemed to be doing its utmost to fling him
off. There came a rattle of crockery from within. Then
suddenly there came another sound from within – a loud,
agonised scream. It was a female scream. Someone who
had been asleep behind the curtain had just awakened.

William's hair stood on end. He almost forgot to cling
to the seat. For not one scream came but many. They rent
the still summer air, mingled with the sound of breaking
glass and crockery. The mule continued his mad career
down the hill, his reins trailing in the dust. In the distance
was a little gipsy's donkey cart full of pots and pans.
William found his voice suddenly and began to warn the
mule.

'Look out, you ole softie,' he yelled. 'Look out for the
donk, you ole ass.'

But the mule refused to be warned. He neatly escaped
the donkey cart himself, but he crashed the caravan into it
with such force that the caravan broke a shaft and over-
turned completely on to the donkey cart, scattering pots
and pans far and wide. From within the caravan came
inhuman female yells of fear and anger. William had
fallen on to a soft bank of grass. He was discovering, to

his amazement, that he was still alive and practically unhurt. The mule was standing meekly by and smiling to himself. Then out of the window of the caravan climbed a woman – a fat, angry woman, shaking her fist at the world in general. Her hair and face were covered with sugar and a fork was embedded in the front of her dress. Otherwise she, too, had escaped undamaged.

The owner of the donkey cart arose from the melee of pots and pans and turned upon her fiercely. She screamed at him furiously in reply. Then along the road could be seen the figure of a fat man carrying a fishing rod. He began to run wildly towards the caravan.

'*Ach! Gott im Himmel!*' he cried as he ran. 'My beautiful caravan! Who has this to it done?'

He joined the frenzied altercation that was going on between the donkey man and the fat woman. The air was rent by their angry shouts. A group of highly appreciative villagers collected round them. Then one of them pointed to William, who sat, feeling still slightly shaken, upon the bank.

'It was 'im wot done it,' he said, 'it was 'im that was a-drivin' of it down the 'ill.'

With one wild glance at the scene of devastation and anger, William turned and fled through the wood.

'*Ach! Gott im Himmel!*' screamed the fat man,

beginning to pursue him. The fat woman and the donkey man joined the pursuit. To William it was like some ghastly nightmare after an evening's entertainment at the cinema.

Meanwhile the donkey and the mule fraternised over the debris and the villagers helped themselves to all they could find. But the fat man was very fat, and the fat woman was very fat, and the donkey man was very old,

WILLIAM'S HAIR STOOD ON END. HE ALMOST FORGOT TO
CLING TO THE SEAT. FOR NOT ONE SCREAM CAME BUT
MANY, MINGLED WITH THE SOUND OF BREAKING GLASS
AND CROCKERY.

and William was young and very fleet, so in less than ten minutes they gave up the pursuit and returned panting and quarrelling to the road. William sat on the further outskirts of the wood and panted. He felt on the whole exhilarated by the adventure. It was quite a suitable adventure for his last day of unregeneration. But he felt also in need of bodily sustenance, so he purchased a bun and a bottle of lemonade at a neighbouring shop and sat by the roadside to recover. There were no signs of his pursuers.

He felt reluctant to return home. It is always well to follow a morning's absence from school by an afternoon's absence from school. A return in the afternoon is ignominious and humiliating. William wandered round the neighbourhood experiencing all the thrill of the outlaw. Certainly by this time the gardener would have complained to his father, probably the schoolmistress would have sent a note. Also – someone had been scratched by the cat.

William decided that all things considered it was best to make a day of it.

He spent part of the afternoon in throwing stones at a scarecrow. His aim was fairly good, and he succeeded in knocking off the hat and finally prostrating the wooden framework. There followed an exciting chase by an angry farmer.

It was after teatime when he returned home, walking with careless bravado as of a criminal who has drunk of crime to its very depth and flaunts it before the world. His spirits sank a little as he approached the gate. He could see through the trees the fat caravan-owner gesticulating at the door. Helped by the villagers, he had tracked William. Phrases floated to him through the summer air.

'Mine beautiful caravan . . . *Ach . . . Gott im Himmel!*'

He could see the gardener smiling in the distance. There was a small blue bruise on his shining head. William judged from the smile that he had laid his formal complaint before authority. William noticed that his father looked pale and harassed. He noticed, also, with a thrill of horror, that his hand was bound up, and that there was a long scratch down his cheek. He knew the cat had scratched *somebody*, but . . . Crumbs!

A small boy came down the road and saw William hesitating at the open gateway.

'*You'll* catch it!' he said cheerfully. 'They've wrote to say you wasn't in school.'

William crept round to the back of the house beneath the bushes. He felt that the time had come to give himself up to justice, but he wanted, as the popular saying is, to be sure of 'getting his money's worth'. There was the tin half full of green paint in the tool shed. He'd had his eye on it

for some time. He went quietly round to the tool shed.
Soon he was contemplating with a satisfied smile a green
and enraged cat and a green and enraged hen. Then, brac-
ing himself for the effort, he delivered himself up to

WILLIAM'S SPIRITS SANK A LITTLE AS HE APPROACHED THE
GATE. HE COULD SEE THROUGH THE TREES THE FAT
CARAVAN-OWNER GESTICULATING AT THE DOOR.

justice. When all was said and done no punishment could be really adequate to a day like that.

Dusk was falling. William gazed pensively from his bedroom window. He was reviewing his day. He had almost forgotten the stormy and decidedly unpleasant scene with his father. Mr Brown's rhetoric had been rather lost on William, because its pearls of sarcasm had been so far above his head. And William had not been really loath to retire at once to bed. After all, it had been a very tiring day.

Now his thoughts were going over some of its most exquisite moments – the moments when the pea and the gardener's head met and rebounded with such satisfactory force; the moment when he swung along the high road, monarch of a caravan and a mule and the whole wide world; the moment when the scarecrow hunched up and collapsed so realistically; the cat covered with green paint . . . After all it was his last day. He saw himself from tomorrow onward leading a quiet and blameless life, walking sedately to school, working at high pressure in school, doing his homework conscientiously in the evening, being exquisitely polite to his family and instructors – and the vision failed utterly to attract. Moreover, he hadn't yet tried turning off the water at the main, or locking the cook into the larder, or – or hundreds of things.

The Reform of William

There came a gentle voice from the garden.

'William, where are you?'

William looked down and met the earnest gaze of Deborah.

'Hello,' he said.

'William,' she said. 'You won't forget that you're going to start tomorrow, will you?'

William looked at her firmly.

'I can't jus' tomorrow,' he said. 'I'm puttin' it off. I'm puttin' it off for a year or two.'

CHAPTER 13

WILLIAM AND THE ANCIENT SOULS

The house next to William's had been unoccupied for several months, and William made full use of its garden. Its garden was in turns a jungle, a desert, an ocean, and an enchanted island. William invited select parties of his friends to it. He had come to look upon it as his own property. He hunted wild animals in it with Jumble, his trusty hound; he tracked Red Indians in it, again with Jumble, his trusty hound; and he attacked and sank ships in it, making his victims walk the plank, again with the help and assistance of Jumble, his trusty hound. Sometimes, to vary the monotony, he made Jumble, his trusty hound, walk the plank into the rain tub. This was one of the many unpleasant things that William brought into Jumble's life. It was only his intense love for William that reconciled him to his existence. Jumble was one of the very few beings who appreciated William.

The house on the other side was a much smaller one, and was occupied by Mr Gregorius Lambkin. Mr Gregorius Lambkin was a very shy and rather elderly bachelor.

William and the Ancient Souls

He issued from his front door every morning at half past eight holding a neat little attaché case in a neatly gloved hand. He spent the day in an insurance office and returned, still unruffled and immaculate, at about half past six. Most people considered him quite dull and negligible, but he possessed the supreme virtue in William's eyes of not objecting to William. William had suffered much from unsympathetic neighbours who had taken upon themselves to object to such innocent and artistic objects as catapults and pea-shooters, and cricket balls. William had a very soft spot in his heart for Mr Gregorius Lambkin. William spent a good deal of his time in Mr Lambkin's garden during his absence, and Mr Lambkin seemed to have no objection. Other people's gardens always seemed to William to be more attractive than his own – especially when he had no right of entry into them.

There was quite an excitement in the neighbourhood when the empty house was let. It was rumoured that the newcomer was a Personage. She was the President of the Society of Ancient Souls. The Society of Ancient Souls was a society of people who remembered their previous existence. The memory usually came in a flash. For instance, you might remember in a flash when you were looking at a box of matches that you had been Guy Fawkes. Or you might look at a cow and remember in a flash that you had been Nebuchadnezzar. Then you joined the Society of Ancient Souls, and paid a large subscription, and attended meetings at the house of its President in costume. And the President was coming to live next door to William. By a curious coincidence her name was Gregoria – Miss Gregoria Mush. William awaited her coming with anxiety. He had discovered that one's next-door neighbours make a great difference to one's life. They may be agreeable and not object to mouth organs and whistling and occasional stone-throwing, or they may not. They sometimes – the worst kind – go to the length of writing notes to one's father about one, and then, of course, the only course left to one is one of Revenge. But William hoped great things from Miss Gregoria Mush. There was a friendly sound about the name. On the evening of her arrival he climbed up on the roller and gazed wistfully over the fence at the territory that had once been his, but from which he was now debarred. He felt like Moses surveying the Promised Land.

Miss Gregoria Mush was walking in the garden. William watched her with bated breath. She was very long, and very thin, and very angular, and she was reading poetry out loud to herself as she trailed about in her long draperies.

' "Oh, moon of my delight . . ." ' she declaimed, then

her eyes met William's. The eyes beneath her pince-nez were like little gimlets.

'How dare you stare at me, you rude boy?' she said.

William gasped.

'I shall write to your father,' she said fiercely, and then proceeded still ferociously, ' ". . . that knows no wane".'

'Crumbs!' murmured William, descending slowly from his perch.

She did write to his father, and that note was the first of many. She objected to his singing, she objected to his shouting, she objected to his watching her over the wall, and she objected to his throwing sticks at her cat. She objected both verbally and in writing. This persecution was only partly compensated for by occasional glimpses of meetings of the Ancient Souls. For the Ancient Souls met in costume, and sometimes William could squeeze through the hole in the fence and watch the Ancient Souls meeting in the dining-room. Miss Gregoria Mush arrayed as Mary, Queen of Scots (one of her many previous existences) was worth watching. And always there was the garden on the other side. Mr Gregorius Lambkin made no objections and wrote no notes. But clouds of Fate were gathering round Mr Gregorius Lambkin. William first heard of it one day at lunch.

'I saw the old luny talking to poor little Lambkin to-

'HOW DARE YOU STARE AT ME, YOU RUDE BOY?' SHE SAID.

day,' said Robert, William's elder brother.

In these terms did Robert refer to the august President of the Society of Ancient Souls.

And the next news Robert brought home was that 'poor little Lambkin' had joined the Society of Ancient Souls, but didn't seem to want to talk about it. He seemed very vague as to his previous existence, but he said that Miss Gregoria Mush was sure that he had been Julius Caesar. The knowledge had come to her in a flash when he raised his hat and she saw his bald head.

There was a meeting of the Ancient Souls that evening, and William crept through the hole and up to the dining-room window to watch. A gorgeous scene met his eye. Noah conversed agreeably with Cleopatra in the window seat, and by the piano Napoleon discussed the Irish ques-tion with Lobengula. As William watched, his small nose flattened against a corner of the window, Nero and Dante arrived, having shared a taxi from the station. Miss Greg-oria Mush, tall and gaunt and angular, presided in the robes of Mary, Queen of Scots, which was her favourite previous existence. Then Mr Gregorius Lambkin arrived. He looked as unhappy as it is possible for man to look. He was dressed in a toga and a laurel wreath. Heat and nervousness had caused his small waxed moustache to droop. His toga was too long and his laurel wreath was crooked. Miss Gregoria Mush received him effusively. She carried him off to a corner seat near the window, and there they conversed, or, to be more accurate, she talked and he listened. The window was open and William could hear some of the things she said.

'Now you are a member you must come here often . . . you and I, the only Ancient Souls in this vicinity . . . we will work together and live only in the Past. . . . Have you remembered any other previous existence? . . . No? Ah, try, it will come in a flash any time . . . I must come and see your garden . . . I feel that we have much in common, you and I . . . We have much to talk about . . . I have all my past life to tell you of . . . What train do you come home by? . . . We must be friends – real friends . . . I'm sure I can help you much in your life as an Ancient Soul . . . Our names are almost the same . . . Fate in some way unites us . . .'

And Mr Lambkin sat, miserable and dejected and yet with a certain pathetic resignation. For what can one do against Fate? Then the President caught sight of William and approached the window.

'Go away, boy!' she called. 'You wicked, rude, prying boy, go away!'

Mr Lambkin shot a wretched and apologetic glance at William, but William pressed his mouth to the open slit of the window.

'All right, Mrs Jarley!' he called, then turned and fled.

William met Mr Lambkin on his way to the station the next morning. Mr Lambkin looked thinner and there were lines of worry on his face.

'I'm sorry she sent you away, William,' he said. 'It must have been interesting to watch – most interesting to watch. I'd much rather have watched than – but there, it's very kind of her to take such an interest in me. *Most* kind. But I – however, she's very kind, *very* kind. She very kindly presented me with the costume. Hardly suitable, perhaps, but *very* kind of her. And, of course, there *may* be something in it. One never knows. I *may* have been Julius Caesar, but I hardly think – however, one must keep an open mind. Do you know any Latin, William?'

'Jus' a bit,' said William, guardedly. 'I've *learnt* a lot, but I don't *know* much.'

'Say some to me. It might convey something to me. One never knows. She seems so sure. Talk Latin to me, William.'

'Hic, haec, hoc,' said William obligingly.

Julius Caesar's reincarnation shook his head.

'No,' he said, 'I'm afraid it doesn't seem to mean anything to me.'

'Hunc, hanc, hoc,' went on William monotonously.

'I'm afraid it's no good,' said Mr Lambkin. 'I'm afraid

it proves that I'm not – still one may not retain a knowledge of one's former tongue. One must keep an open
mind. Of course, I'd prefer not to – but one must be fair.
And she's kind, very kind.'

MR LAMBKIN SAT, MISERABLE AND DEJECTED, AND YET
WITH A CERTAIN PATHETIC RESIGNATION.

Shaking his head sadly, the little man entered the station.

That evening William heard his father say to his mother:

'She came down to meet him at the station tonight. I'm afraid his doom is sealed. He's no power of resistance, and she's got her eye on him.'

'Who's got her eye on him?' said William with interest.

'Be quiet!' said his father with the brusqueness of the male parent.

But William began to see how things stood. And William liked Mr Lambkin.

One evening he saw from his window Mr Gregorius Lambkin walking with Miss Gregoria Mush in Miss Gregoria Mush's garden. Mr Gregorius Lambkin did not look happy.

William crept down to the hole in the fence and applied his ear to it.

They were sitting on a seat quite close to his hole.

'Gregorius,' the President of the Society of Ancient Souls was saying, 'when I found that our names were the same I knew that our destinies were interwoven.'

'Yes,' murmured Mr Lambkin. 'It's so kind of you, so kind. But – I'm afraid I'm overstaying my welcome. I must—'

'No. I must say what is in my heart, Gregorius. You live in the Past, I live in the Past. We have a common mission – the mission of bring to the thoughtless and uninitiated the memory of their former lives. Gregorius, our work would be more valuable if we could do it together, if the common destiny that has united our nomenclatures could unite also our lives.'

'It's so *kind* of you,' murmured the writhing victim, 'so kind. I am so unfit, I—'

'No, friend,' she said kindly. 'I have power enough for both. The human speech is so poor an agent, is it not?'

A doorbell clanged in the house.

'Ah, the Committee of the Ancient Souls. They were coming from town tonight. Come here tomorrow night at the same time, Gregorius, and I will tell you what is in my heart. Meet me here – at this time – tomorrow evening.'

William here caught sight of a stray cat at the other end of the garden. In the character of a cannibal chief he hunted the white man (otherwise the cat) with blood-curdling war-whoops, but felt no real interest in the chase. He bound up his scratches mechanically with an ink-stained handkerchief. Then he went indoors. Robert was conversing with his friend in the library.

'Well,' said the friend, 'it's nearly next month. Has she landed him yet?'

'By Jove!' said Robert. 'First of April tomorrow!' He looked at William suspiciously. 'And if you try any fool's tricks on me you'll jolly well hear about it.'

'I'm not thinkin' of you,' said William crushingly. 'I'm not goin' to trouble with *you*!'

'Has she landed him?' said the friend.

'Not yet, and I heard him saying on the train that he was leaving town on the second and going abroad for a holiday.'

'Well, she'll probably do it yet. She's got all the first.'

'It's bedtime, William,' called his mother.

'Thank heaven!' said Robert.

William sat gazing into the distance, not seeing or hearing.

'*William!*' called his mother.

'All right,' said William irritably. 'I'm jus' thinkin' something out.'

William's family went about their ways cautiously the next morning. They watched William carefully. Robert even refused an egg at breakfast because you never knew with that little wretch. But nothing happened.

'Fancy your going on April Fool's day without making a fool of anyone,' said Robert at lunch.

'It's not over, is it? Not yet,' said William with the air of a sphinx.

'But it doesn't count after twelve,' said Robert.

William considered deeply before he spoke, then he said slowly:

'The thing what I'm going to do counts whatever time it is.'

Reluctantly, but as if drawn by a magnet, Mr Lambkin set off to the President's house. William was in the road.

'She told me to tell you,' said William unblushingly, 'that she was busy tonight, an' would you mind not coming.'

The tense lines of Mr Lambkin's face relaxed.

'Oh, William,' he said, 'it's a great relief. I'm going away early tomorrow, but I was afraid that tonight—' he was almost hysterical with relief. 'She's so kind, but I was afraid that – well, well, I can't say I'm sorry – I'd promised to come, and I couldn't break it. But I was afraid – and I hear she's sold her house and is leaving in a month, so – but she's kind – *very* kind.'

He turned back with alacrity.

'Thanks for letting me have the clothes,' said William.

'Oh, you're quite welcome, William. They're nice things for a boy to dress up in, no doubt. I can't say I – but she's *very* kind. Don't let her see you playing with them, William.'

William grunted and returned to his back garden.

For some time silence reigned over the three back gardens. Then Miss Gregoria Mush emerged and came towards the seat by the fence. A figure was already seated there in the half dusk; a figure swathed in a toga with the toga drawn also over its drooping head.

'Gregorius!' said the President. 'How dear of you to come in costume!'

The figure made no movement.

'You know what I have in my heart, Gregorius?'

Still no answer.

'Your heart is too full for words,' she said kindly. 'The thought of having your destiny linked with mine takes speech from you. But have courage, dear Gregorius. You shall work for me. We will do great things together. We will be married at the little church.'

Still no answer.

'Gregorius!' she murmured tenderly:

She leant against him suddenly, and he yielded beneath the pressure with a sudden sound of dissolution. Two cushions slid to the ground, the toga fell back, revealing a broomstick with a turnip fixed firmly to the top. It bore the legend:

APRIL FOOL

And from the other side of the fence came a deep sigh of satisfaction from the artist behind the scenes.

'GREGORIUS,' SAID THE PRESIDENT. 'HOW DEAR OF YOU TO COME IN COSTUME!' THE FIGURE MADE NO MOVEMENT.

CHAPTER 14

WILLIAM'S CHRISTMAS EVE

It was Christmas. The air was full of excitement and secrecy. William, whose old-time faith in notes to Father Christmas sent up the chimney had died a natural death as the result of bitter experience, had thoughtfully presented each of his friends and relations with a list of his immediate requirements.

He had a vague and not unfounded misgiving that his family would begin at the bottom of the list instead of the top. He was not surprised, therefore, when he saw his father come home rather later than usual carrying a parcel of books under his arm. A few days afterwards he announced casually at breakfast.

'Well, I only hope no one gives me *The Great Chief*, or *The Pirate Ship*, or *The Land of Danger* for Christmas.'

His father started.

'Why?' he said sharply.

'Jus' 'cause I've read them, that's all,' explained William with a bland look of innocence.

The glance that Mr Brown threw at his offspring was

not altogether devoid of suspicion, but he said nothing. He set off after breakfast with the same parcel of books under his arm and returned with another. This time, however, he did not put them in the library cupboard, and William searched in vain.

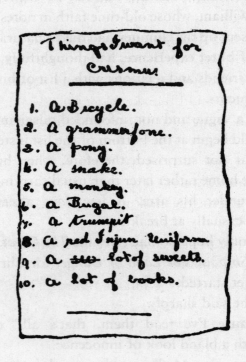

Things I want for Crismus

1. A Bicycle.
2. A grammerfone.
3. A pony.
4. A snake.
5. A monkey.
6. A Bugal.
7. A trumpit
8. A red Injun Uniform
9. A lot of sweets.
10. A lot of books.

William's Christmas Eve

The question of Christmas festivities loomed large upon the social horizon.

'Robert and Ethel can have their party on the day before Christmas Eve,' decided Mrs Brown, 'and then William can have his on Christmas Eve.'

William surveyed his elder brother and sister gloomily.

'Yes, an' us eat up jus' what they've left,' he said with bitterness. '*I* know!'

Mrs Brown changed the subject hastily.

'Now let's see whom we'll have for your party, William,' she said, taking out pencil and paper. 'You say whom you'd like and I'll make you a list.'

'Ginger an' Douglas an' Henry and Joan,' said William promptly.

'Yes? Who else?'

'I'd like the milkman.'

'You can't have the milkman, William. Don't be so foolish.'

'Well, I'd like to have Fisty Green. He can whistle with his fingers in his mouth.'

'He's a butcher's boy, William! You *can't* have him.'

'Well, who *can* I have?'

'Johnnie Brent?'

'I don't like him.'

'But you must invite him. He asked you to his.'

237

'Well, I didn't want to go,' he said irritably, 'you made me.'

'But if he asks you to his you must ask him back.'

'You don't want me to invite folks I don't *want*?' William said in the voice of one goaded against his will into exasperation.

'You must invite people who invite you,' said Mrs Brown firmly; 'that's what we always do at parties.'

'Then they've got to invite you again and it goes on and on and *on*,' argued William. 'Where's the *sense* of it? I don't like Johnnie Brent an' he don't like me an' if we go on inviting each other an' our mothers go on making us go, it'll go on and on and *on*. Where's the *sense* of it? I only jus' want to know where's the *sense* of it?'

His logic was unanswerable.

'Well, anyway, William, I'll draw up the list. You can go and play.'

William walked away, frowning, with his hands in his pockets.

'Where's the *sense* of it?' he muttered as he went.

He began to wend his way towards the spot where he, and Douglas, and Ginger, and Henry met daily in order to while away the hours of the Christmas holidays. At present they lived and moved and had their being in the characters of Indian Chiefs.

As William walked down the back street, which led by a short cut to their meeting place, he unconsciously assumed an arrogant strut, suggestive of some warrior prince surrounded by his gallant braves.

'Garn! *Swank!*'

He turned with a dark scowl.

On the doorstep sat a little girl, gazing up at him with blue eyes beneath a tousled mop of auburn hair.

William's eyes travelled sternly from her Titian curls to her bare feet. He assumed a threatening attitude and scowled fiercely.

'You better not say *that* again,' he said darkly.

'Why not?' she said with a jeering laugh.

'Well, you'd just better *not*,' he said with a still more ferocious scowl.

'What'd you do?' she persisted.

He considered for a moment in silence. Then: 'You'd see what I'd do!' he said ominously.

'Garn! *Swank!*' she repeated. 'Now do it! Go on, do it!'

'I'll – let you off *this* time,' he said judicially.

'Garn! *Softie*. You can't do anything, you can't! You're a softie!'

'I could cut your head off an' scalp you an' leave you hanging on a tree, I could,' he said fiercely, 'an' I will, too, if you go on calling me names.'

'*Softie! Swank!* Now cut it off! Go on!'

He looked down at her mocking blue eyes.

'You're jolly lucky I don't start on you,' he said threateningly. 'Folks I do start on soon get sorry, I can tell you.'

'What do you do to them?'

He changed the subject abruptly.

'What's your name?' he said.

'Sheila. What's yours?'

'Red Hand – I mean, William.'

'I'll tell you sumpthin' if you'll come an' sit down by me.'

'What'll you tell me?'

'Sumpthin' I bet you don't know.'

'I bet I *do*.'

'Well, come here an' I'll tell you.'

He advanced towards her suspiciously. Through the open door he could see a bed in a corner of the dark, dirty room and a woman's white face upon the pillow.

'Oh, come *on*!' said the little girl impatiently.

He came and sat down beside her.

'Well?' he said condescendingly. 'I bet I knew all the time.'

'No, you didn't! D'you know,' she sank her voice in a confidential whisper, 'there's a chap called Father Christmas wot comes down chimneys Christmas Eve and leaves presents in people's houses?'

He gave a scornful laugh.

'Oh, that *rot*! You don't believe *that* rot, do you?'

'Rot?' she repeated indignantly. 'Why, it's *true – true* as *true*! A boy told me wot had hanged his stocking up by the chimney an' in the morning it was full of things an' they was jus' the things wot he'd wrote on a bit of paper an' thrown up the chimney to this 'ere Christmas chap.'

'Only *kids* believe that rot,' persisted William. 'I left off believin' it years and *years* ago!'

Her face grew pink with the effort of convincing him.

'But the boy *told* me, the boy wot got things from this 'ere chap wot comes down chimneys. An' I've wrote wot I want an' sent it up the chimney. Don't you think I'll get it?'

William looked down at her. Her blue eyes, big with apprehension, were fixed on him, her little rosy lips were parted. William's heart softened.

'I dunno,' he said doubtfully. 'You might, I s'pose. What d'you want for Christmas?'

'You won't tell if I tell you?'

'No.'

'Not to no one?'

'No.'

'Say, "Cross me throat".'

'GARN! *SWANK!*' WILLIAM TURNED WITH A DARK SCOWL.

William complied with much interest and stored up the phrase for future use.

'Well,' she sank her voice very low and spoke into his ear.

'Dad's comin' out Christmas Eve!'

She leant back and watched him, anxious to see the effect of this stupendous piece of news. Her face expressed pride and delight. William's merely bewilderment.

'Comin' out?' he repeated. 'Comin' out of where?'

Her expression changed to one of scorn.

'*Prison*, of course! *Silly!*'

William was half offended, half thrilled.

'Well, I couldn't *know* it was prison, could I? How could I *know* it was prison without bein' told? It might of been out of anything. What' – in hushed curiosity and awe – 'what was he in prison for?'

'Stealin'.'

Her pride was unmistakable. William looked at her in disapproval.

'Stealin's wicked,' he said virtuously.

'Huh,' she jeered, 'you *can't* steal! You're too soft! *Softie!* You *can't* steal without bein' copped fust go, you can't.'

'I *could*!' he said indignantly. 'And, anyway, he got

copped, di'n't he? Or he'd not of been in prison, *so there!*'

'He di'n't get copped fust go. It was jus' a sorter mistake, he said. He said it wun't happen again. He's a jolly good stealer. The cops said he was and *they* oughter know.'

'Well,' said William changing the conversation, 'what d'you want for Christmas?'

'I wrote it on a bit of paper an' sent it up the chimney,' she said confidingly. 'I said I di'n't want no toys nor sweeties nor nuffin'. I said I only wanted a nice supper for Dad when he comes out Christmas Eve. We ain't got much money, me an' Mother, an' we carn't get 'im much of a spread, but – if this 'ere Christmas chap sends one fer 'im, it'll be – *fine!*'

Her eyes were dreamy with ecstasy. William stirred uneasily on his seat.

'I tol' you it was *rot*,' he said. 'There isn't any Father Christmas. It's jus' an' ole tale folks tell you when you're a kid, an' you find out it's not true. He won't send no supper jus' 'cause he isn't anythin'. He's jus' nothin' – jus' an ole tale—'

'Oh, shut *up!*' William turned sharply at the sound of the shrill voice from the bed within the room. 'Let the kid 'ave a bit of pleasure lookin' forward to it, can't yer? It's little enough she 'as, anyway.'

William arose with dignity.

'All right,' he said. 'Go'bye.'

He strolled away down the street.

'*Softie!*'

It was a malicious sweet little voice.

'*Swank!*'

William flushed but forbore to turn round.

That evening he met the little girl from next door in the road outside her house.

'Hello, Joan!'

'Hello, William!'

In these blue eyes there was no malice or mockery. To Joan William was a godlike hero. His very wickedness partook of the divine.

'Would you – would you like to come an' make a snowman in our garden, William?' she said tentatively.

William knit his brows.

'I dunno,' he said ungraciously. 'I was jus' kinder thinkin'.'

She looked at him silently, hoping that he would deign to tell her his thoughts, but not daring to ask. Joan held no modern views on the subject of the equality of the sexes.

'Do you remember that ole tale 'bout Father Christmas, Joan?' he said at last.

245

She nodded.

'Well, s'pose you wanted somethin' very bad, an' you believed that ole tale and sent a bit of paper up the chimney 'bout what you wanted very bad and then you never got it, you'd feel kind of rotten, wouldn't you?'

She nodded again.

'I did one time,' she said. 'I sent a lovely list up the chimney and I never told anyone about it and I got lots of things for Christmas and not *one* of the things I'd written for!'

'Did you feel awful rotten?'

'Yes, I did. Awful.'

'I say, Joan,' he said importantly, 'I've gotter secret.'

'*Do* tell me, William!' she pleaded.

'Can't. It's a crorse-me-throat secret!'

She was mystified and impressed.

'How *lovely*, William! Is it something you're going to do?'

He considered.

'It might be,' he said.

'I'd love to help.' She fixed adoring blue eyes upon him.

'Well, I'll see,' said the lord of creation. 'I say, Joan, you comin' to my party?'

'Oh, *yes*!'

'Well, there's an awful lot comin'. Johnnie Brent an' all

that lot. I'm jolly well not lookin' forward to it, I can *tell* you.'

'Oh, I'm so sorry! Why did you ask them, William?'

William laughed bitterly.

'Why did I invite them?' he said. '*I* don't invite people to my parties. *They* do that.'

In William's vocabulary 'they' always signified his immediate family circle.

William had a strong imagination. When an idea took hold upon his mind, it was almost impossible for him to let it go. He was quite accustomed to Joan's adoring homage. The scornful mockery of his auburn-haired friend was something quite new, and in some strange fashion it intrigued and fascinated him. Mentally he recalled her excited little face, flushed with eagerness as she described the expected spread. Mentally also he conceived a vivid picture of the long waiting on Christmas Eve, the slowly fading hope, the final bitter disappointment. While engaging in furious snowball fights with Ginger, Douglas, and Henry, while annoying peaceful passers-by with well-aimed snow missiles, while bruising himself and most of his family black and blue on long and glassy slides along the garden paths, while purloining his family's clothes to adorn various unshapely snowmen, while walking across all the ice (preferably cracked) in the neighbourhood and being several times narrowly rescued from a watery grave – while following all these light holiday pursuits, the picture of the little auburn-haired girl's disappointment was ever vividly present in his mind.

The day of his party drew near.

'*My* party,' he would echo bitterly when anyone of his family mentioned. 'I don't *want* it. I don't *want* ole Johnnie Brent an' all that lot. I'd just like to uninvite 'em all.'

'But you want Ginger and Douglas and Henry,' coaxed his mother.

'I can have them any time an' I don't like 'em at parties. They're not the same. I don't like *anyone* at parties. I don't *want* a party!'

'But you *must* have a party, William, to ask back people who ask you.'

William took up his previous attitude.

'Well, where's the *sense* of it?' he groaned.

As usual he had the last word, but left his audience unconvinced. They began on him a full hour before his guests were due. He was brushed and scrubbed and scoured and cleaned. He was compressed into an Eton suit and patent leather pumps and finally deposited in the drawing-room, cowed and despondent, his noble spirit all but broken.

The guests began to arrive. William shook hands

politely with three strangers shining with soap, brushed to excess, and clothed in ceremonial Eton suits – who in ordinary life were Ginger, Douglas, and Henry. They then sat down and gazed at each other in strained and unnatural silence. They could find nothing to say to each other. Ordinary topics seemed to be precluded by their festive appearance and the formal nature of the occasion. Their informal meetings were usually celebrated by impromptu wrestling matches. This being debarred, a stiff, unnatural atmosphere descended upon them. William was a 'host', they were 'guests'; they had all listened to final maternal admonitions in which the word 'manners' and 'politeness' recurred at frequent intervals. They were, in fact, for the time being, complete strangers.

Then Joan arrived and broke the constrained silence.

'Hullo, William! Oh, William, you do look *nice*!'

William smiled with distant politeness, but his heart warmed to her. It is always some comfort to learn that one has not suffered in vain.

'How d'you do?' he said with a stiff bow.

Then Johnnie Brent came and after him a host of small boys and girls.

William greeted friends and foes alike with the same icy courtesy.

Then the conjurer arrived.

Mrs Brown had planned the arrangement most carefully. The supper was laid on the big dining-room table. There was to be conjuring for an hour before supper to 'break the ice'. In the meantime, while the conjuring was going on, the grown-ups who were officiating at the party were to have their meal in peace in the library.

William had met the conjurer at various parties and despised him utterly. He despised his futile jokes and high-pitched laugh and he knew his tricks by heart. They sat in rows in front of him – shining-faced, well-brushed little boys in dark Eton suits and gleaming collars, and dainty white-dressed little girls with gay hair ribbons. William sat in the back row near the window, and next to him sat Joan. She gazed at his set, expressionless face in mute sympathy. He listened to the monotonous voice of the conjurer.

'Now, ladies and gentlemen, I will proceed to swallow these three needles and these three strands of cotton and shortly to bring out each needle threaded with a strand of cotton. Will any lady step forward and examine the needles? Ladies ought to know all about needles, oughtn't they? You young gentlemen don't learn to sew at school, do you? Ha! Ha! Perhaps some of you young gentlemen don't know what a needle is! Ha! Ha!'

William scowled, and his thoughts flew off to the little house in the dirty back street. It was Christmas Eve. Her father was 'comin' out'. She would be waiting, watching with bright, expectant eyes for the 'spread' she had demanded from Father Christmas to welcome her returning parent. It was a beastly shame. She was a silly little ass, anyway, not to believe him. He'd told her there wasn't any Father Christmas.

'Now, ladies and gentlemen, I will bring out the three needles threaded with the three strands of cotton. Watch carefully, ladies and gentlemen. There! One! Two! Three! Now, I don't advise you young ladies and gentlemen to try this trick. Needles are very indigestible to some people. Ha! Ha! Not to me, of course! I can digest anything – needles, or marbles, or matches, or glass bowls – as you will soon see. Ha! Ha! Now to proceed, ladies and gentlemen.'

William looked at the clock and sighed. Anyway, there'd be supper soon, and that was a jolly good one, 'cause he'd had a look at it.

Suddenly the inscrutable look left his countenance. He gave a sudden gasp and his whole face lit up. Joan turned to him.

'Come on!' he whispered, rising stealthily from his seat.

The room was in half darkness and the conjurer was just producing a white rabbit from his left toe, so that few

251

noticed William's quiet exit by the window followed by
that of the blindly obedient Joan.

'You wait!' he whispered in the darkness of the garden.
She waited, shivering in her little white muslin dress, till he
returned from the stable wheeling a handcart, consisting

FEW NOTICED WILLIAM'S EXIT BY THE WINDOW, FOLLOWED
BY THE BLINDLY OBEDIENT JOAN.

of a large packing case on wheels and finished with a handle. He wheeled it round to the open French window that led into the dining-room. 'Come on!' he whispered again.

Following his example, she began to carry the plates of sandwiches, sausage rolls, meat pies, bread and butter, cakes and biscuits of every variety from the table to the handcart. On the top they balanced carefully the plates of jelly and blancmange and dishes of trifle, and round the sides they packed armfuls of crackers.

At the end she whispered softly, 'What's it for, William?'

'It's the secret,' he said. 'The crorse-me-throat secret I told you.'

'Am I going to help?' she said in delight.

He nodded.

'Jus' wait a minute,' he added, and crept from the dining-room to the hall and upstairs.

He returned with a bundle of clothing which he proceeded to arrange in the garden. He first donned his own red dressing gown and then wound a white scarf round his head, tying it under his chin so that the ends hung down.

'I'm makin' believe I'm Father Christmas,' he deigned to explain. 'An' I'm makin' believe this white stuff is hair an' beard. An' this is for you to wear so's you won't get cold.'

He held out a little white satin cloak edged with swansdown.

'Oh, how *lovely*, William! But it's not my cloak! It's Sadie Murford's!'

'Never mind! You can wear it,' said William generously.

Then, taking the handle of the cart, he set off down the drive. From the drawing-room came the sound of a chorus of delight as the conjurer produced a goldfish in a glass bowl from his head. From the kitchen came the sound of the hilarious laughter of the maids. Only in the dining-room, with its horrible expanse of empty table, was silence.

They walked down the road without speaking till Joan gave a little excited laugh.

'This is *fun*, William! I do wonder what we're going to do.'

'You'll see,' said William. 'I'd better not tell you yet. I promised a crorse-me-throat promise I wouldn't tell anyone.'

'All right, William,' she said sweetly. 'I don't mind a bit.'

The evening was dark and rather foggy, so that the strange couple attracted little attention, except when passing beneath the street lamps. Then certainly people stood still and looked at William and his cart in open-mouthed amazement.

At last they turned down a back street towards a door that stood open to the dark, foggy night. Inside the room was a bare table at which sat a little girl, her blue, anxious eyes fixed on the open door.

'I hope he gets here before Dad,' she said. 'I wouldn't like Dad to come and find it not ready!'

The woman on the bed closed her eyes wearily.

'I don't think he'll come now, dearie. We must just get on without it.'

The little girl sprang up, her pale cheek suddenly flushed.

'Oh, *listen*,' she cried; '*something's* coming!'

They listened in breathless silence, while the sound of wheels came down the street towards the empty door. Then – an old handcart appeared in the doorway and behind it William in his strange attire, and Joan in her fairy-like white – white cloak, white dress, white socks and shoes – her dark curls clustered with gleaming fog jewels.

The little girl clasped her hands. Her face broke into a rapt smile. Her blue eyes were like stars.

'Oh, oh!' she cried. 'It's Father Christmas and a fairy!'

Without a word William pushed the cart through the

doorway into the room and began to remove its contents and place them on the table. First the jellies and trifles and blancmanges, then the meat pies, pastries, sausage rolls, sandwiches, biscuits, and cakes – sugar-coated, cream-interlayered, full of plums and nuts and fruit. William's mother had had wide experience and knew well what food

FIRST THE JELLIES AND BLANCMANGES – THEN THE
MEAT PIES AND TRIFLES.

most appealed to small boys and girls. Moreover, she had provided plentifully for her twenty guests.

The little girl was past speech. The woman looked at them in dumb wonder. Then:

'Why, you're the boy she was talkin' to,' she said at last. 'It's real kind of you. She was gettin' that upset. It 'ud have broke her heart if nothin' had come an' I couldn't do nothin'. It's real kind of yer, sir!' Her eyes were misty.

Joan placed the last cake on the table, and William, who was rather warm after his exertions, removed his scarf.

The child gave a little sobbing laugh.

'Oh, isn't it *lovely*? I'm so happy! You're the funny boy, aren't you, dressed up as Father Christmas? Or did Father Christmas send you? Or were you Father Christmas all the time? May I kiss the fairy? Would she mind? She's so beautiful!'

Joan came forward and kissed her shyly, and the woman on the bed smiled unsteadily.

'It's real kind of you both,' she murmured again.

Then the door opened, and the lord and master of the house entered after his six months' absence. He came in no sheepish hangdog fashion. He entered cheerily and boisterously as any parent might on returning from a hard-earned holiday.

' 'Ello, Missus! 'Ello, Kid! 'Ello! Wot's all this 'ere?' His eyes fell upon William. ''Ello, young gent!'

'Happy Christmas,' William murmured politely.

'Sime to you an' many of them. 'Ow are you, Missus? Kid looked arter you all right? That's *right*. Oh, I *sye*! Where's the grub come from? Fair mikes me mouth water. I 'aven't seen nuffin' like *this* – not fer *some* time!'

There was a torrent of explanations, everyone talking at once. He gave a loud guffaw at the end.

'Well, we're much obliged to this young gent and this little lady, and now we'll 'ave a good ole supper. This is all *right*, this is! Now, Missus, you 'ave a good feed. Now, 'fore we begin, I sye three cheers fer the young gent and little lady. Come on, now, 'Ip, 'ip, 'ip, '*ooray*! Now, little lady, you come 'ere. That's fine, that is! Now 'oo'll 'ave a meat pie? 'Oo's fer a meat pie? Come on, Missus! That's right. We'll *all* 'ave meat pie! This 'ere's sumfin *like* Christmas, eh? We've not 'ad a Christmas like this – not for many a long year. Now, 'urry up, Kid. Don't spend all yer time larfin. Now, ladies an' gents, 'oo's fer a sausage roll? All of us? Come on, then! I mustn't eat too 'eavy or I won't be able to sing to yer arterwards, will I? I've got some fine songs, young gent. And Kid 'ere'll dance fer yer. She's a fine little dancer, she is! Now, come on, ladies an' gents, sandwiches? More pies? Come on!'

They laughed and chattered merrily. The woman sat up in bed, her eyes bright and her cheeks flushed. To William and Joan it was like some strange and wonderful dream.

And at that precise moment Mrs Brown had sunk down upon the nearest dining-room chair on the verge of tears, and twenty pairs of hungry horrified eyes in twenty clean, staring, open-mouthed little faces surveyed the bare expanse of the dining-room table. And the cry that went up all round was:

'*Where's William?*'

And then:

'*Where's Joan?*'

They searched the house and garden and stable for them in vain. They sent the twenty enraged guests home supperless and aggrieved.

'Has William eaten *all* our suppers?' they said.

'Where *is* he? Is he dead?'

'People will never forget,' wailed Mrs Brown. 'It's simply dreadful. And where *is* William?'

They rang up police stations for miles around.

'If they've eaten all that food – the two of them,' said Mrs Brown almost distraught, '– they'll *die*! They may be dying in some hospital now! And I do wish Mrs Murford would stop ringing up about Sadie's cloak. I've told her it's not here!'

Meantime there was dancing, and singing, and games, and cracker-pulling in a small house in a back street not very far away.

'I've never had such a *lovely* time in my life,' gasped the Kid breathlessly at the end of one of the many games into which William had initiated them. 'I've never, never, *never*—'

'We won't ferget you in a 'urry, young man,' her father added, 'nor the little lady neither. We'll 'ave many talks about this 'ere!'

Joan was sitting on the bed, laughing and panting, her curls all disordered.

'I wish,' said William wistfully, 'I wish you'd let me come with you when you go stealin' some day!'

'I'm not goin' stealin' *no* more, young gent,' said his friend solemnly. 'I got a job – a real steady job – bricklayin', an' I'm goin' to stick to it.'

All good things must come to an end, and soon William donned his red dressing gown again and Joan her borrowed cloak, and they helped to store the remnants of the feast in the larder – the remnants of the feast would provide the ex-burglar and his family with food for many days to come. Then they took the empty handcart and, after many fond farewells, set off homeward through the dark.

Mr Brown had come home and assumed charge of operations.

Ethel was weeping on the sofa in the library.

'Oh, dear little William!' she sobbed. 'I do *wish* I'd always been kind to him!'

Mrs Brown was reclining, pale and haggard, in the armchair.

'There's the Roughborough Canal, John!' she was saying weakly. 'And Joan's mother will always say it was our fault. Oh, *poor* little William!'

'It's a good ten miles away,' said her husband drily. 'I don't think even William—' He rang up fiercely. 'Confound these brainless police! Hello! Any news? A boy and girl and supper for twenty can't disappear off the face of the earth. No, there had been *no* trouble at home. There probably *will* be when he turns up, but there was none before! If he wanted to run away, why would he burden himself with a supper for twenty? Why – one minute!'

The front door opened and Mrs Brown ran into the hall.

A well-known voice was heard speaking quickly and irritably.

'I jus' went away, that's all! I jus' thought of something I wanted to do, that's all! Yes, I *did* take the supper. I jus' wanted it for something. It's a secret what I wanted it for, I—'

'*William!*' said Mr Brown.

Through the scenes that followed William preserved a dignified silence, even to the point of refusing any explanation. Such explanation as there was filtered through from Joan's mother by means of the telephone.

'It was all William's idea,' Joan's mother said plaintively. 'Joan would never have done *anything* if William hadn't practically *made* her. I expect she's caught her death of cold. She's in bed now—'

'Yes, so is William. I can't *think* what they wanted to take *all* the food for. And he was just a common man straight from prison. It's dreadful. I do hope they haven't picked up any awful language. Have you given Joan some quinine? Oh, Mrs Murford's just rung up to see if Sadie's cloak has turned up. Will you send it round? I feel so *upset* by it all. If it wasn't Christmas Eve—'

The house occupied by William's and Joan's

'WASN'T SHE A JOLLY LITTLE KID?' WILLIAM SAID EAGERLY.

families respectively were semi-detached, but William's and Joan's bedroom windows faced each other, and there was only about five yards between them.

There came to William's ears as he lay drowsily in bed the sound of a gentle rattle at the window. He got up and opened it. At the opposite window a little white-robed figure leant out, whose dark curls shone in the starlight.

'William,' she whispered, 'I threw some beads to see if you were awake. Were your folks mad?'

'Awful,' said William laconically.

'Mine were too. I di'n't care, did you?'

'No, I di'n't. Not a bit!'

'William, wasn't it *fun*? I wish it was just beginning again, don't you?'

'Yes, I jus' do. I say, Joan, wasn't she a jolly little kid and di'n't she dance fine?'

'Yes,' – a pause – then, 'William, you don't like her better'n me, do you?'

William considered.

'No, I don't,' he said at last.

'YES.' A PAUSE, THEN – 'WILLIAM, YOU DON'T LIKE HER BETTER'N ME, DO YOU?'

263

A soft sigh of relief came through the darkness.

'I'm so *glad*! Go'night, William.'

'Go'night,' said William sleepily, drawing down his window as he spoke.

THE END

JUST
WILLIAM

RICHMAL CROMPTON

WITH A FOREWORD BY SUE TOWNSEND

'He's mad,' said Mr Brown with conviction. 'Mad. It's the only explanation.'

There's only one William Brown – better known as Just William. Whether he's trying to arrange a marriage for his sister or taking a job as a bootboy as step one in his grand plan to run away, William manages to cause chaos wherever he goes.

WILLIAM
AGAIN

RICHMAL CROMPTON

WITH A FOREWORD BY LOUISE RENNISON

'*Me?*' *said William in horror.* '*I've not done any-thing.*'

Totally bankrupt, William and Ginger can't even buy sweets. But then William has a brilliant idea – they could sell Ginger's twin cousins as slaves! Before long, the irrepressible William is in serious trouble – again . . .

WILLIAM
THE FOURTH

RICHMAL CROMPTON

WITH A FOREWORD BY FRANK COTTRELL BOYCE

'He's – he's more like a nightmare than a boy.'

Whether he's occupying a bear suit that's slightly too small for him, cloaked in mystery as a fortune-teller or attired in the flowing robes of a Fairy Queen, William is unmistakably himself: trouble in human form. Only Great-Aunt Jane manages to take William on at his own game – and win!

STILL
WILLIAM

RICHMAL CROMPTON

WITH A FOREWORD BY TONY ROBINSON

'If all girls are like that –' said William. 'Well, when you think of all the hundreds of girls there must be in the world – well, it makes you feel sick.'

William's natural desire to do the right thing leads him into serious trouble, as usual, and when blackmail and kidnapping are involved, it's no surprise. Even when he turns over a new leaf, the consequences are dire. But it's his new neighbour Violet Elizabeth Bott who really causes chaos – and no one will believe that it's not William's fault . . .

WILLIAM
AT WAR

Richmal Crompton

With a foreword by Charlie Higson

'Your nuisance value is so high I'm sure you're the last person Hitler would wish to bomb.'

William is always ready to offer his services to his country. But his enthusiastic contribution is seldom appreciated. Determined to do his bit, William soon proves himself just as dangerous, unpredictable and downright troublesome as the Enemy!

GIS, Environmental Modelling and Engineering